Timberman Werebear

(Saw Bears, Book 3)

T. S. JOYCE

Timberman Werebear

ISBN-13: 978-1537786957
ISBN-10: 1537786954
Copyright © 2015, T. S. Joyce
First electronic publication: March 2015

T. S. Joyce
www.tsjoyce.com

NOTE FROM THE AUTHOR:
This book is a work of fiction. The names, characters, places, and incidents are products of the writer's imagination or have been used fictitiously and are not to be construed as real. Any resemblance to persons, living or dead, actual events, locale or organizations is entirely coincidental. The author does not have any control over and does not assume any responsibility for third-party websites or their content.

Published in the United States of America

First digital publication: March 2015
First print publication: September 2016

Editing: Corinne DeMaagd

ONE

Danielle Clayton had made the worst decision of her life moving back to Saratoga.

That awful choice was highlighted by the man sitting on the stage across the bar in a halo of blinding spotlight taking a long pull of what was likely a whiskey and coke as he prepared to perform his next song.

How did she know it was a whiskey and coke? Because she knew him as well as anyone could get to know a sack of secrets like Denison Beck. Charming, funny, entirely comfortable under scrutiny, outspoken, mouthy red-blooded man. All the outer attributes he allowed people to see. Attributes that made people feel like they knew him when they really didn't know him at all.

Denison Beck was an enigma. Always had been, always would be.

She cast a lingering glance over her shoulder as his darker haired twin brother, Brighton, strummed the first chord of the next song. Sounded like it would be a country crooner. Denison looked different than he had four years ago. He'd lost the lankiness of boyhood and grown short, dark scruff on his face. Probably intentional and not from laziness. Denison had been a perfectionist when she'd had cause to know him on a personal level. At least he seemed to be from the few times she was allowed to visit his meticulously tidy home, back when they were dating.

As Denison pressed the frets of his guitar with long, graceful fingers, his bicep bulged under the dark green T-shirt that clung to his defined musculature like a second skin. Gym rat. She'd forgotten to add gym rat to his list of known qualities. And sex pot.

She took a sip of her cranberry vodka and tried to yank her gaze away from his flexing pec as he strummed along with Brighton. Nope. Her eyes refused, the traitors, and traveled down to his powerful legs, bent at the knee as he settled into his rhythm on the old bar stool. Even the holes in his jeans had probably been bought that way. She couldn't imagine him looking like a slouch without purpose. But it wasn't his demigod body that had slayed her all those years ago. It had been his eyes. Under the designer-messy sandy-brown crop of hair, his eyes were soft and gray as he belted out the first lyric in that deep, rich baritone that used to make her ovaries explode. The trio of ladies at the next table sighed in unison, then leaned closer.

"Aw, for crap's sake," she muttered and dragged her attention back to her drink. She wasn't going to be one of his groupies. Not this time around.

This time, she was here for a job. That was all.

Her hands shook, and she checked the door once more. If Darren didn't show in three minutes, she was out of here. It was cruel to expect her to sit here and listen to her ex sing songs about a love he knew nothing about. And Darren, that little piss-ant, was half an hour late. It was his idea to have a business meeting at a bar, and he'd just so happened to pick Denison's old haunt. Admittedly, she had hoped to enjoy some fond memories here tonight, not see her danged ex doing what he'd probably been doing the entire four years she'd been away at school—singing at Sammy's Bar and banging locals.

Freaking Denison. He'd never change. Which made her take a long, head-clearing pull of air and nod her head at how justified she had been in leaving his ass. Except in her bout of self-righteousness, she inhaled the plume of a passerby's exhaled cigarette smoke and coughed in the most unattractive snort she'd ever heard come from a woman. Lovely.

Time to go. She stood, but a tall man with piercing blue eyes blocked her way.

"Leavin' so soon?" he asked in a thick drawl.

She smiled politely and took a final sip of her drink, then set the glass on the table with a clunk. "I've been here long enough. 'Scuse me."

"Let me buy you another drink," the man said. "My name's Matt, and I've been watching you sitting over here by yourself. I came here alone tonight, too, so I get it."

"Get what?" 'Cause she sure as snickers didn't need a man right now, if that was what he was implying. She especially didn't need one to pity flirt with her to make her feel like she wasn't just some loser sitting alone in a bar.

Matt lowered his head and voice. "I get that you came here looking for a...connection."

She screwed up her lips and swallowed a giggle. "Connection, no. Stiff drink, yes." And a meeting with that little weasel Darren before he headed into the wilderness on his own. "I'm just going to close out my tab and be on my way."

He snatched her cell phone from her hand and typed in a number, then saved it to her contacts, the ass. "So, what's your name?" he asked with a cool, playboy smile.

His teeth were blinding white, like he'd bleached them with household cleaners. She couldn't take her eyes away from them. His feline grin was like a bug light, calling to her.

Completely uninterested in getting to know more about Matt and his eye-scorching grill, she ducked around him and leaned onto the bar top. The bartender was busy with a buxom blonde down the counter. Meanwhile, Denison's voice hit the slower last notes of the song. Panic constricted Danielle's throat. *He can't see me*, she reminded herself. The spotlight ensured Denison couldn't see anyone past the first few tables from the stage. She was safe all the way over here in the shadow of Matt the flirty giant.

Matt's hips brushed her backside, and she jerked forward.

"Let me take care of this one," he said, his lips so close to her ear his voice vibrated through her.

His arms propped against the counter on either side of her, trapping her. With a gasp, Danielle rounded on him. "Back. The fuck. Off." Claustrophobia was going to give her a full-blown, double ball-kicking panic fit right here in the middle of this smoky joint.

She tried to duck under his arm, but he moved to block her with his massive, muscled torso.

"My girl here needs another drink," Matt called down the bar.

"I'm not your girl," she gritted out, measuring the distance she would need to drive a knee into his groin if he didn't move. Damn her stumpy, short legs.

Matt bowed forward, the smell of alcohol pungent on his breath. Danielle leaned back as far as the bar top would allow her, but it wasn't enough.

She was pushing his immovable chest now, angling her face away from his as he zeroed in on her lips.

"Stop it," she demanded, just as his lips brushed the corner of her mouth.

Matt's shoulder jerked backward, and he spun away from her. The wide expanse of Denison's shoulders now blocked Matt from view.

"Oh, shit," she murmured. Frantically, she flagged down the bartender, kicking herself for not paying in cash. When she turned to her right, Brighton was sitting on the bar stool next to her, sipping a beer like he'd been there all night. "Double shit," she said, leaning her head back and closing her eyes.

With a sigh, she opened them again, just as recognition flashed across his green eyes. He didn't look any happier about her being here than she was. "Hey Brighton. Good to see you again."

Brighton leaned back, exposing the thick cords of muscle in his neck and his bulging Adam's apple. He pulled a pen from his pocket and wrote a hurried scribble across a napkin as Denison bullied Matt out the front door.

She stared down at the napkin Brighton shoved

in front of her. He didn't talk. Never had from what she understood, and if he wanted to say anything, he wrote it.

You're gonna hurt him.

The words cut her deeper than she thought possible. They also confused the devil out of her. Hurt him? That was practically laughable. Ha, ha, ha, hurt *him*. Denison was an invincible and unfeeling razor blade who'd shredded her when they'd split up.

Brighton's dark eyebrows lifted, and he shook his head, as if she were in it now, better dig in her heels.

"You okay, lady?" Denison asked in that familiar baritone she'd fallen in love with.

The voice that had made her feel things no one else had.

The voice that probably made lots of women feel lots of things.

She wasn't special.

"I'm fine." Tears stung her eyes and red bubbled through her veins at the idea she was melting down in front of the man who'd destroyed her. With a tentative smile for the bartender who handed her back her credit card, she signed for a tip, dodged around Denison with her chin lowered to her chest, and made a bee-line for the door.

She passed so close to him, she could hear him inhale sharply.

"Danielle?"

Yep, it was definitely time to go. She'd known she would run into him in Saratoga. In fact, it would be necessary for her to complete what she'd come here to do, but it wasn't supposed to happen now. She had planned to swoop in here, settle in, maybe make some local friends, and throw herself into work. She had wanted to deal with the avalanche of memories before she tried to talk to Denison, preferably without a tremor in her voice. She'd be straight-up damned if she was going to converse with him all weak and teary. Nope, nope, nope.

"Hey, Danielle," Denison called from right behind her.

She pushed her legs harder, realized the two double cranberry vodkas she'd slurped down had affected her more than she thought, and promptly tripped over the door stop. With a squelch, she lurched forward and landed on her hands on the unforgiving cement. Good thing she'd worn a hoochie skirt tonight and banged up her knees to match her scraped palms. Pain shot up the nerve endings of her scuffed up skin.

And now the waterworks were unstoppable as embarrassment blasted heat up her neck and into her cheeks. As she looked up, she was mortified to find Denison crouching in front of her, hands out as if he didn't know what to do to help her, a horrified look on his face.

"Are you okay?" he asked.

"I'm fantastic," she said around a sob. "I'm just…" She struggled upward and wiped her bleeding hands on her skirt. "I'm just wonderful."

"Here, don't do that. It'll hurt worse." Denison held her hands in his and studied her palms.

And to her utter annoyance and dismay, her body reacted to him, just as it had those years ago. From where he touched her, tingling warmth ran up her arms. It pooled at her shoulders, then flowed into her chest and down into her quivering belly. He looked up with a startled look in his gray eyes—eyes that seemed lighter than she remembered.

"You feel it, too," he accused.

Anger snapped her spine straight, and she yanked her hands from his. "I don't feel anything." Ignoring her stupid tears that stained her stupid cheeks in stupid rivers, she stomped around him and tossed her purse into the passenger seat of her open-doored jeep, then slid behind the wheel.

"You can't just leave without telling me why," Denison said, suddenly at her door.

"Why what?" she said, swallowing her anguish.

"Why did you leave without saying anything? You were supposed to be here, with me, for three more days before you went back to school. Dammit, Danielle," he said, clenching his fists on either side of her door. His voice dipped to a ragged whisper. "I was supposed to have three more days."

She huffed and shook her head slowly. Why? Because he'd invited her to watch him play a show, and when she'd come to meet up with him, he had his arms around another woman. His lips on another woman. She closed her eyes against the pain of his betrayal. "You really can't think of any reason why I would've left without saying goodbye?" *You cheating rat.*

15

Denison looked at her like he was lost and swallowed hard. "No."

The look on his face, so raw and open, nearly doubled her over. Her chest hurt more than her scraped hands and knees. "I can't do this right now."

"Danielle—"

"I can't! I'm not ready for this conversation. I'm sorry I ever came back." She jammed the key and turned the engine, then pulled through an empty parking space and sped off.

She looked in the rearview mirror just once. Denison was standing in the middle of the gravel parking lot with his fingers linked behind his head, chin tilted back, agony written across his face.

Danielle had made the worst decision of her life moving back to Saratoga.

TWO

In utter shock, Denison stood in the half-empty parking lot of Sammy's bar eating a cloud of Danielle's dust and wondering what the hell had just happened. Four years without a peep from the woman, and all the sudden, she was back, riling up his bear just like she had once upon a time. He ran his hands up the back of his scalp and flung them in front of him.

He'd almost gotten over her.

Brighton snickered a silent laugh from beside him like he'd heard his lying thoughts.

"Shut up, man," Denison grumbled to his brother.

Of course Brighton would find this amusing. He'd sworn off a mate since he was a cub. Denison had played that game until he'd met Danielle, fresh out of her first year of college for the summer, working an internship for some environmentalist group up in the mountains near Saratoga.

One summer, and his bear had chosen. Too bad she hadn't chosen him back.

Denison bit back a curse and twitched his head. "Let's grab our stuff and get out of here." Preferably before that asshat Matt came back with a couple of his Gray Back buddies and began a crew on crew brawl in a parking lot of inebriated humans.

Matt Barns was an old not-friend and definitely due for an ass-kicking, but not here, and not tonight.

The toe of Denison's work boot faltered on a stone sticking out of the gravel, and he fought the urge to rip it from the ground and chuck it against the lone tree that sat between here and the main drag in town.

Four years ago, he'd imagined meeting up with Danielle again. After a few months with no word from her, he'd known she wasn't ever coming back. She'd gone back to college and begun a new life that didn't include him. But that hadn't stopped him from visualizing what one more hour with her would be like, what he would ask, and if she still loved him. Well, apparently he'd done something wrong, but damned if he knew what. "Freakin' women."

"You done for the night?" Ted, the bartender, asked.

"Yeah, we're gonna cut out early. We're gonna try to beat rush-hour."

Ted chuckled at the joke and waved them off. Rush hour didn't exist here in this small town, and it sure wasn't a problem out on the winding road from here to the Asheland Mobile Park where he and Brighton lived. The worst traffic he ever found was a family of raccoons taking their sweet-ass time to cross the road on occasion, but other than that, he was lucky to pass another car on the two-hour drive back.

Denison picked up his guitar from where it sat leaning crooked against his chair. He wasn't usually rough with his instruments, and especially not his favorite guitar, but when he'd heard the ruckus near the bar and squinted through the blinding stage lights to see Matt messing with another townie, well, he'd nearly lost it trying to get to her. That guy spelled trouble every time he came in here looking for an easy lay. He was never subtle about his intentions, and when he was rejected, which was often, he wasn't very gracious about it.

"You okay to drive?" Ted asked as Denison packed his guitar in an old, scratched-up case.

"Old man, you know I don't drink too much when I have a show. Brighton had a beer, but I'm driving." His whiskey and coke was all for show. If he nursed a drink all night, the ladies laid off buying him more.

"It's habit to ask," Ted called, wiping down the counter. "Same time next week?"

"You bet."

The conversation went like this every week, on repeat for five years. Denison's inner animal required a strict routine. Work until his bones were sore on the jobsite as a timber man, indulge in the company of his crew in the evenings, sleep a full eight hours, then do it all again. And on Friday, it was gig time at Sammy's Bar. Good gravy, life was boring, but it was what his bear needed, so fine.

He lifted his gaze to the road Danielle had disappeared down in that sexy, forest green, jacked-up jeep she'd been driving. Life hadn't been boring the summer she'd been here.

She looked different now. Her hair used to be long, down to her hips, and as dark as raven feathers. It was still dark, but only fell to her shoulder blades now, and she wore it in soft curls instead of straight. He liked it. She still had those fiery almond-colored eyes, pert little nose and tiny, elfin lips that he wanted to suck swollen, but as far as he remembered, she'd never worn a short skirt in front of him. Not until tonight. She hadn't the confidence to dress like that when he'd known her before. Or *thought* he'd known her.

Brighton clapped him on the back so hard it rattled his innards. Right. Back to earth. He settled the guitar case in the back of his old beat-up Bronco and slid behind the wheel. His brother was grinning from ear to ear by the time the engine roared to life.

"What?" Denison asked.

Brighton lifted his eyebrows and shrugged.

"Did you like that little show? Me running after her like a puppy, making a fool of myself? Well," he said, backing out of the parking space Ted had reserved for *talent* with a hand-painted sign, "I feel like grit now."

The two-hour trip back was brutal on account of Brighton leaning back the seat and promptly falling asleep, leaving Denison to try and stay awake without company the entire drive through the mountains. Which meant two hours of summer-kissed, swimming-hole memories with Danielle. He'd watched her open up that season, from a timid bookworm to a woman. He'd thought she was forever, but he'd been wrong. And now, the same devastating hole that had sat in his stomach for a year after she left was back, eating him from the inside out. God, he wished she would have just stayed away. That look on her face when she was crying in the parking lot, like he'd killed her kitten... How was he supposed to get that vision out of his head? Her face all crumpled and tears streaking her cheeks, making dark smudges of sadness under her eyes. And her hands...Dammit, he'd had to fight not to Change and clean her wounds. Her knees had been trickling red, but she didn't seem to care at all. All she seemed to care about was getting as far away from him as she could.

He'd replayed their last day together over and

over, but he still couldn't figure out what he'd done to piss her off so badly that she'd leave and never come back. Never call or write, or hell, send a damned carrier pigeon. Poof! She just vanished, leaving his bear unmanageable and littering his chest cavity with little shredded pieces of his heart.

And that was the autumn he had sworn off women forever. Brighton had the right of it all along. Don't let women get close, and they couldn't hurt him. Not like Danielle had. Never again.

When he finally pulled under the Asheland Mobile Park sign at the entrance of a double row of trailers the Ashe crew inhabited, he was just about dead on his feet.

Brighton stumbled off to his own house without so much as a wave, and Denison dragged his guitar case up the porch stairs and inside his trailer. He poured a drink from the tap, but the water was a little on the brown side from the pipes not being used all day, so he dumped the glass and let the sink run for a minute before he tried again. Tasted a little dirty, but Dad always said that a little grit in his food would put hair on a man's chest. Whatever that meant. From his experience, women didn't much prefer heavy pelts.

Danielle had preferred him smooth when they'd gotten to the bedding portion of their relationship. He remembered the way she'd run her hands across his torso, petting him and tethering his animal to her even more, like some spell caster securing his bond. She'd had soft hands compared to his calloused ones. And incredible tits. All round with those perfect pink nipples drawing up hard anytime his lips touched them and... Shit. His dick was already swollen and thumping against the seam of his pants.

Denison chugged the water and rinsed the glass. It did no good thinking about her finer qualities. It just made the hole in the pit of his stomach yawn open a little wider. He wouldn't ever have her again. That much was clear from the way she had looked at him when she'd been in the jeep. Like it hurt to lay her eyes on him.

He jerked open the drawer of odds and ends and dug through to the back before finding what he was looking for. Three photographs were all he had of his time with Danielle. He hadn't looked at them in three years on principle. He wiped dust off a close-up picture of her kissing his cheek as he smiled at the camera. The second was of Danielle swinging on an old tire he'd tied from a giant pine tree in the backyard of the cabin he'd shared with Brighton at the time. Bright red gloss painted her lips, and she wore a matching knee-length summer dress that billowed out as she swung. Fucking gorgeous. The third had been his favorite, though. It was of her and Brighton leaned back on their elbows in tall meadow grass, lying in the sun with their eyes closed and heads tossed back. She wore a white sundress with little cherries on it. He traced the arc of her neck with his fingertip and grimaced at the pain in his chest.

Then he thought about burning the pictures over the stove, like he had contemplated doing a hundred times. Maybe if they didn't exist anymore, if they didn't sit in that drawer haunting him, maybe the pain would stop and he could forget about her. But just like every other time, he decided against it. If he got rid of the only thing he had left of her, he'd be truly alone. And that seemed somehow worse than the pain of losing her.

Whatever reason she'd thought of to come back, he wished she'd hurry up and leave so he could start getting over her again.

****

An ear-splitting racket filled Danielle's ears, and she hunched in on herself. When she was buried deep within the warm wrinkles of her blanket, she cracked an eye open. The noise began again. She lurched up and tossed the covers away from her. The cell phone clattered across the tiny nightstand by her bed as it screamed again. Why the devil had she picked that hideous ring tone?

"Hello," she croaked into the receiver.

"Ms. Clayton," Mr. Reynolds purred. "Are we still asleep?"

"Uhh." She squinted at the blurry, battery-operated alarm clock next to her bed. "Not anymore. I thought I wasn't starting until Monday."

"I assume you've settled in nicely to the rental I've given to you?"

She looked around the swanky, refurbished Airstream RV and nodded a tangled lock of hair out of her face. "Yes, sir, I have. It's much nicer than I imagined it would be when you hired me."

"Good. Then you won't mind starting your research a little bit early. I'm on a bit of a time crunch, I'm afraid."

"To discover the solution for the beetle

infestation?" It was definitely going to take more than two extra days to solve the fiasco that had killed off the trees in the area.

"Your counterpart, Darren, is already on his way into the wilderness as we speak. Do take his enthusiasm and allow it to affect yours."

"Sir, I'm very enthusiastic about this job. I'm sorry for the miscommunication, but I specifically remember you saying I was to start on Mon—"

"Ms. Clayton," Reynolds snapped. "I have no patience for excuses. If you want this job, and if you want to be paid for this job, you will start today." He sighed into the phone. "Now that we have that cleared up, I've decided to partner you with someone who knows the area."

"Wait, what? This was supposed to be a lone job, and we were supposed to exchange notes in weekly meetings to bring you our findings. Darren and I can cover more ground if we work separately."

"I didn't say anything about you working with Darren. You're to be working with Denison Beck. I've been told you're already familiar with him."

Her mouth dropped open, and she frowned so hard her face hurt. Nope. Hell no to that. She scrunched up her nose and closed her eyes to ward away the oncoming headache Mr. Reynolds was proving to be. "I'm not working with that man. He holds no value to the job I'm doing, and we don't get along. If I must work with someone, fine. Choose anyone on the planet besides him. Please."

"You seem to think this is a suggestion. It's not. I'll text you the address you are to meet him at and any pertinent information. Have him show you around his territory."

"His territory? Excuse me for asking, but what does that mean? He's a townie."

"Not anymore."

Danielle viciously fought the urge to strangle the phone. She gritted her teeth so hard, her jaw hurt, then tried again. "Mr. Reynolds, I've been very excited about joining in on this research for you, but this wasn't part of the job description."

"Are you backing out?"

"No. Maybe." She flopped back on the bed in a star-like shape. "Can I have until Monday, my original start-date, to decide on whether to continue with your request? Denison and I have history. The relationship is complicated, and I hadn't expected to spend any substantial amount of time with him."

Another long, irritated sigh blasted across the phone speaker. "That would be fine."

"One last thing," she rushed out before he hung up. "Does Denison work for you?"

"No. Not directly."

"Then how do you know he'll help me?"

"Because, Ms. Clayton, I have a feeling you can be very compelling when you want to be."

The line went dead, and she glared at the screen until it went blank.

A screech of pure frustration rattled her throat, and she stared at the low ceiling above her. She'd have to pull out of the job, and the trip would be wasted because there was no way in hades she was signing up for hours, days, and possibly weeks in the woods with Denison-the-man-ho-Beck.

THREE

Denison was dog tired. The kind of exhausted that seeped into his bones and made him want to sleep for a full twenty-four hour block of time. He'd focused on work today to keep his mind off Danielle. He'd spent half the night awake, wondering if he'd dreamed her at Sammy's, but from the concerned look on his brother's face this morning, she'd definitely been there.

Brighton worried too damned much. He waffled between finding amusement in Denison's love life—or lack thereof—to fretting like a mother hen that Danielle was going to break him in half again. Well, she wasn't. Denison wasn't going to let her get that close. He'd even protected himself by calling up to Sammy's and cancelling his gig next weekend, so there was no chance of seeing her in town since he wouldn't be there. Sure, he and the boys were headed up to the Lumberjack Wars competition the newly opened sawmill in Saratoga had organized, but it was off in the woods and miles away from a risk of running into her.

His Bronco lurched side to side as he maneuvered around a pair of potholes so deep he could probably spit in them and hit magma. Last week's rains had washed out the roads worse than they usually were. He was caked in dirt and sweat, and his muscles twitched from the exertion of working every daylight hour with his crew, trying to keep on top of lumber deadlines so they could give themselves enough time to take a day off tomorrow and escort the girls, Brooke and Skyler, to their first lumberjack competition.

Drew was laid out like a corpse in the back seat, snoring softly with his yellow hardhat draped over his face, and Brighton stared out the window in the passenger's seat as Denison followed Kellen's white lifted pickup truck down the rugged terrain back toward Asheland Mobile Park. Home was situated in the valley between this mountain and the next. Through the tinted window ahead, he could make out Kellen and his mate, Skyler, as they tipped their heads together for a kiss.

Denison dragged his gaze back to the dirt road disappearing under the nose of his Bronco. Their affection had never bothered him before, but it was different now with all his emotions stirred up by Danielle's unexpected arrival in town. He gripped the wheel and clenched his teeth. There she was again, clouding his mind with memories of those sexy lips and how good they'd tasted when he'd been lucky enough to have her.

He turned the radio dial to the only radio station out here that got reception, and an old rock-n-roll classic blared through the speakers. Brighton tossed him the fiftieth worried look for the day, and Denison considered booting him from the Bronco and making his ass walk the rest of the way home. Pitying looks made his bear want to kill things.

By the time he pulled through the back gate behind the other trucks, Brighton had wisely decided to ignore him and keep his attention out the window.

"Drew, wake up," he muttered as he pulled in front of his trailer. "We're home."

Denison didn't wait for the others to get out of his ride. It wasn't like he needed to lock his doors around here, so he took his porch steps two-by-two and left them to get out as slowly as they wanted.

He hung his hardhat by the door and stripped his shirt and work boots off on the way to his bedroom. Before the tap was even steaming, he was under the cool jets of water, letting it rinse streams of mud down his torso and arms.

He was a happy person by nature, but ever since last night, he'd been feeling off. It was as if a huge gaping hole had opened in his chest, growing bigger and bigger until it threatened to swallow up the good parts about him. That's what love had done to him. That's why he would never allow that worthless emotion to taint him again. Tagan had found his mate in Brooke, and Kellen had found Skyler, but that didn't mean every grizzly shifter found a partner. They were the exception to the rule. Most stayed in bachelor groups, fucked humans when the need to mate became too much, and went their entire lives without finding a true mate. Lady bear shifters were rare. Not many survived in vitro, and Turning women was frowned upon. If women weren't strong enough, and dominant enough, their inner grizzlies would maim them from the inside out.

He'd messed up with Danielle—allowed himself to bond with her. Allowed his grizzly to choose a fragile human as a potential mate, when he should have been bedding her, then running for the hills like every other male of his kind would've done. Well, maybe not every male. He thought of Kellen and Tagan and how they lived and breathed to make their mates happy. Hell, Denison loved Brooke and Skyler like they were his own blood-siblings and would die for either one of them without hesitation. And damn it all, a greedy, needy, pathetic little part of him wanted what Tagan and Kellen had. He wanted to feel like they did and have his devotion returned.

Danielle was a runner, though. History proved it, and she had shown him she hadn't changed one bit when she took off last night in a plume of tire grit.

With a growl, he forced her from his mind and concentrated on soaping his body. Of course, he was then contending with his raging boner that seemed to spring to life whenever he thought of Danielle, but as tempting as it was to take himself in hand and stroke out a release, the knot of tension would no doubt still be in his shoulders after he emptied himself into the water running down the drain. Plus, now that Danielle was back in his life and sexier than ever, a steamy shower jack-off session just didn't seem as fulfilling as it had two days ago.

He pressed the palms of his hands against the cool plastic shower tiles and glared at the cracked grout between. She'd ruined everything.

With a sigh, he hit the faucet and stepped out of the shower, then promptly ignored his two day scruff. From what he remembered, Danielle hadn't liked to kiss him when he wasn't clean shaven. He'd rubbed her raw with a couple of marathon make-out sessions, one of which had led to the first time he'd slipped his finger into her. And there was his dick again, making a tent of his towel. With a growl, he flipped off the razor that sat waiting on the rim of his sink and headed for the bedroom.

He couldn't stomp his feet in here like he was tempted to do, on account he'd probably fall through the squishy spots in the old laminate flooring. He yanked open the top drawer of his dresser to make up for it, then dressed in a huff.

The shower was supposed to reinstate his happy demeanor, but it had failed miserably. Tagan and Brooke were cooking for the crew tonight, though, and if his sniffer wasn't lying, that was spaghetti and garlic bread he smelled wafting through the drafty windows of his trailer.

By the time he made his way outside and down the porch steps, the Ashe crew was gathered around the fire pit at the end of the road. He shook out the last of the water drops from his hair and mussed the top, then jogged toward the others. His shoulders relaxed as he settled into an eye-scorching green plastic lawn chair by the fire with his plate piled high with pasta, mixed vegetables, and finger-singeing hot garlic bread. Leaning over, he grabbed a beer from the red cooler between him and Brighton, and handed his brother one, too. Tops popped, he clinked his bottle against his brother's in silent cheers like Dad had always done before every meal when they were growing up. Then he took a long swig and dug in.

It was amazing how a satisfied stomach after a

hard day of work could change his mood. It was that or the banter of his crew that made for an easy distraction. Kellen wrapped his arm around his passing mate's waist and pulled Skyler into his lap, then whispered something into her ear, causing her to giggle.

Denison smiled at the easy love they'd found and took another pull on his beer. Leaning back, he arched his neck toward the sky and stared at the slashes of airplane contrails that crisscrossed the summer sky.

"What the hell is that?" Bruiser asked.

Denison snapped his head down and frowned at the giant, shiny, silver RV bumping toward the trailer park. And hauling that highfalutin home on wheels was none other than Danielle's green jeep.

"Shee-yit," Denison drawled, sitting forward and draping his elbows on his knees. He needed about a dozen more beers to deal with whatever hell was headed his way.

"Is that..." Tagan squinted at the jeep. "Is that Danielle?"

"Badger's back?" Bruiser crowed.

Kellen was staring over his mate's shoulder at

the approaching vehicle with a calculating look that said he was just going to be a casual observer and not get involved, but Skyler gave a tentative wave to the approaching vehicle from his lap. Out of all of them, she was probably the nicest.

Danielle waved back. She braked and turned off the car, then slid out in what had to be the tightest pair of jeans ever constructed. They clung to her curves in a way that made his belly tighten and his balls swell. Denison would've given his least favorite nut to peel those off her and see if she still liked shaving her lady parts like she used to. Damn, he regretted his decision not to jerk off in the shower.

Haydan whistled, so Denison whacked his knuckles into the guy's stomach. Haydan *oofed* air, and his stupid catcall got stuck in his throat. Served him right.

"Hi, fellas," Danielle called as she sauntered toward the fire.

"Hey, Badger," Drew called out, waggling his blond eyebrows. "What are you doing way out in our neck of the woods?"

"Oh, geez, no one has called me Badger in so long. Drew, Kellen, Haydan, Bruiser, Tagan." She greeted his friends with a smile. She waved to Brighton and introduced herself to Brooke and Skyler, and never once did that stunning grin fade from her face. Not until her eyes landed on Denison.

He swallowed the pain and stood. "Sit on down. You hungry?"

"I don't want to take your food—"

"Nonsense," Kellen said, canting his head at their visitor. "You're Denison's mate. Our food is yours."

"Kellen," Denison gritted out.

Skyler turned and cupped her mate's cheeks, then shook her head and kissed him sweetly on the lips.

"I'm your mate?" Danielle looked partly baffled and entirely uncomfortable with that wordage.

"You remember Kellen," Denison explained. "He don't say things like other people do. I'll get you a plate."

God, he wished the whole damned crew hadn't been around to witness his downward spiral after Danielle left. They'd all been big fans of hers, once upon a time. From the way Haydan was grinning like an idiot, as if he was enjoying the show, Denison suspected maybe they still thought she was all right.

Fan-friggin-tastic.

****

Danielle was wearing her poker face as best as she could, but inside, she was shaking like a leaf in a windstorm. Memories of days at the lake with this wild batch of boys—now men—had her feeling like she was home in a place she'd never seen before. Four years ago, they'd lived all over and around Saratoga, only coming together when someone was throwing a keg party in an overgrown field, or for night-muddin', or Friday nights at Sammy's bar to watch Denison and Brighton play, or really any excuse for them to get together. Through the years, she had thought about the men around the fire who talked to her now like she'd never left. But she'd imagined they'd all moved on and made something of themselves. She most definitely didn't envision them forming some kind of moonshiner commune in the middle of the wilderness. From where she stood, none of them had changed. Not one little bit.

And Denison... God, her heart lurched into her throat, constricting her windpipe until her chest hurt to draw breath. He was beautiful, if a manly woodsman could be called that. Hair damp like he'd just showered, threadbare black shirt holding onto his broad shoulders, and that sexy scruff he wore on his face now. She hadn't ever been attracted to men with facial hair, but damn, could Denison wear it. He was all sex appeal and dove-colored smoldering eyes as he watched her warily. He sat the edge of his seat like he would bolt at any moment, and when he offered her his chair, she thought he'd do just that. Instead, he piled spaghetti and fixings on a plate and offered it to her at arm's length, as if he were afraid she might try to touch him.

"Thank you," she murmured.

The moment was so surreal she had to anchor herself in it so she wouldn't think it was a dream come tomorrow. She clenched her hands until her nails pressed painfully against her palms to remind herself this was really happening. All of these familiar faces and personalities...and Denny. Shit. She blinked rapidly to stop the stupid burning sensation behind her eyes. She hadn't thought of him as Denny in a long time. Anger had made her heart tuck away the term of endearment. She blamed the boys for calling her Badger again.

"Where did you get the nickname?" the blond

woman with open, smiling blue eyes asked.

"Uh, Denny came up with it."

Denison snapped his head up, and Danielle closed her eyes, furious with herself for letting his nickname slip. "What I meant to say is, Denison gave it to me a long time ago."

"On account of her being tenacious," Drew said with a shit-stirring smile. "She followed *Denny* around town to all his gigs for three weeks, quietly stalking him until he was so head over heels in l—"

"That's good," Denison said, his furious gaze dipping to the toe of his boots as he leaned against a make-shift buffet table made of rough, unstained wood.

"Wait, you and Denison dated?" Brooke asked, eyes round as a disbelieving smile crooking her lips.

Danielle was going to kill Mr. Reynolds. Slowly. "Yes," she choked out, then cleared her throat. "For a minute."

"Can I talk to you?" Denison ground out. "Alone?"

"Probably best." Danielle set her plate on her seat and followed Denison's receding back.

He didn't stop until he reached a trailer with the number 1015 over the door. He scaled the porch stairs and threw open the screen door, which banged closed right in front of her.

"Sorry," he muttered as he pushed it open again and waved her inside.

The entryway led to a small living area off an even smaller kitchen. Everything was clean and tidy, in its place. "Is this your house?"

"Yeah," he said, throwing his hands up. "And now you're here in my place making it smell like you so that I'll literally never be able to escape you. So this was an awful idea on my part, bringing you in here."

"Do you want me to leave?"

"Yes, Danielle." Denison gripped his hips and sighed, then turned his back on her and ran his hands through his hair. "And no. I don't know." He collapsed onto a couch that sat in the middle of the living room, long legs folded and knees spread wide. "Why are you here?"

Honesty was best. "I'm here for a job. I was told this morning my job now depends on you."

"On me? What kind of job?"

"I graduated in December and started combing job listings for something in my field. The beetle infestation has been a problem up here, and some big-wig wants research done on the effects on the land around here. He hired me and one other person, Darren, to begin our research to tell him just how badly the area is affected, and to try to come up with solutions that will preserve the ecosystem here. Apparently, I need a guide."

"Can't do it."

Danielle took a seat on the brown micro-suede loveseat that sat next to the couch and asked, "Why not?"

"Because it's you. Do you really think it's a smart idea for us to spend time together? You couldn't stand to be around me for five minutes yesterday before running off. I know the area, but this is fire and gasoline, Danielle. I don't think we should mix them, if you know what I mean. And anyway, I'm on a tight deadline with my crew, and Tagan isn't going to be able to spare me. Best you go and find someone you have a shot at not hating at the end of the day. Someone who has more time and energy for whatever hunt for an ecosystem beetle cure you're on. It ain't me you want for this little adventure. Tell your boss I'm sorry, but the answer is no."

FOUR

Disappointment and relief swirled through her chest as she let his answer wash over her. He'd denied her. It had been a monstrous mountain to climb just to work up the courage to come here tonight, but at least she'd tried. Environmentalists didn't find steady work easily, and especially not jobs that were offering to pay what Reynolds had, but was it worth feeling the depth of the pain she and Denison had caused each other?

Denison couldn't hold her gaze and cracked his knuckles softly against the heavy silence in the room.

She thought not. Nothing was worth this kind of

pain that was slashing through her insides, and from the way Denison's eyebrows drew down, and his eyes dimmed, she wasn't the only one hurt by this reunion.

"I'm sorry I came." She shrugged, unsure of how to word the mass of emotion roiling against her chest cavity. "I didn't mean to hurt either one of us. I just...Well, it doesn't matter."

"You just what?" Denison lifted his eyes slowly to hers, held her gaze, and wouldn't release her.

She dug deep for the bravery she'd grown since she'd left here those years ago. "When I took the job, I was scared you would still be here. And then I was scared you had moved on and I'd never get closure. It's been a confusing month, preparing to come back here."

"Why'd you leave in the first place?" His voice sounded raw and unused, but his eyes stayed steady on her.

"I didn't want to be someone's second choice. I'd thought we were more, but you didn't feel the same."

Denison linked his hands behind his neck and leaned back against the plush couch cushion. "How can you sit there and look me in the eyes and say that? I was willing to give up everything for you. I was scared as shit about what was happening between us, but I was still willing to try and keep you."

"Keep me?"

"Yeah, keep you! Keep you happy, keep you with me. Keep you here. I knew you had to go back to school, and I wasn't going to stand in the way of your education. I saw how much working in the woods meant to you. But I wanted the relationship, even if it was just summers and holidays together, I would've waited. I wanted you to come back to me when you were through. Instead, you just bailed. You never answered my calls, probably shredded my letters. And for what? Because you thought I didn't care about you enough? I cared about you too much."

Heartbreak hunched her forward and a sob clawed its way up her throat. "Then why did you cheat on me?"

Denison froze, eyes wide and furious, mouth set in a thin, shocked line. Slowly, his eyebrows raised. "Cheat on you? And who is it you think I cheated on you with? That's not even an option for my kind, Danielle! Not when we're in that deep. I didn't want anyone else."

Danielle shook her head and shot him a warning look. "Don't." Of course he'd deny it. All men did after they were caught. The walls came for her when she stood, collapsing by inches until they threatened to snuff her out completely.

"Oh, yeah," Denison said, standing. "Run. Run when it gets hard. See, this is why we wouldn't have ever worked. As soon as you get scared, you bolt. If a conversation turns too serious, you disappear like you never freaking existed. Have I ever walked away from talking to you?"

Danielle reached for the doorknob and clutched the cold metal in her damp palm. Tears rimmed her eyes, threatening to overflow. How mortifying that he'd snuffed out all her bravado with a few words.

"No," she whispered. "You never did that." Inhaling deeply, she turned, but was unable to meet his gaze. "I saw you that night. You'd invited me to your show, and I had all these plans."

"What plans?"

"I was going to tell you I loved you that night. I'd felt it for a while, and I'd never said it to anyone, and you'd been saying it for weeks, but I hadn't been able to accept that you could feel that way about someone like me."

"Someone like you. How did you see yourself?"

"The same way everyone saw me. Brainy, unsocial, awkward. But you made me feel pretty and special and cared for, and I wanted to finally tell you how I felt. But you were with *her*." She dared a look at him.

He was shaking his head with his palms open as he approached her like a rancher soothing a spooked horse. "Her who?"

"The redhead. You had your arms around her, and you were both smiling and whispering in each other's ears. And then…" She swallowed down the yellow bellied chicken in her. "And then I saw you kiss her."

"Laura?"

"Sure. Great. Now I know her name. At least it's not Cinnamon the whore-faced, nipple clamped, smelly vag—"

"Laura Beck. My sister."

"Oooh."

His sister.

His freaking sister?

No way did Danielle make that big of a mistake. No way did she throw away a relationship with Denny because she was too caught up in being hurt to confront him. The door was smooth against her back as she slid down and pulled her knees to her chest. That certainly put a different spin on how she'd seen him that night. Maybe the embraces hadn't been as flirty as she'd imagined. "Please tell me you're kidding."

"What, you'd rather I cheated on you?"

"Well, I'd been trying for three months to get you to open up to me, and you hadn't given me anything. You didn't talk about your family, you didn't talk about why Brighton doesn't have a voice, you were always meeting up with the boys and sharing all these secret little looks every time I asked a question, and it left me on the outside. You with that girl, cheating on me...well...it made sense why you wouldn't let me in. She made everything make sense." Danielle bit her lip hard to keep another round of tears at bay.

Denison ran his hand roughly through his hair. He picked up a throw pillow, as if he were going to throw it at the wall, but decided against it and yelled into it instead. When he lifted his gaze back to hers, his eyes were blazing a lighter color, as if the shitty fluorescent lighting above him reflected off his face at a strange angle. "Dammit, Danielle, all you had to do was confront me. Literally, all you had to do was pick up your damned cell phone one of the hundred times I called you and let me explain. I knew you were feeling like an outsider. Don't you think I could tell that? I was hurting you, but it was either let you all the way into my life, which included the scary parts, or cut you loose to spare you. I was going to let you know how I felt that night, too. My mom and dad don't live around here, but Laura lives up in Denver. I asked her to drive out here to meet you. That was a big step for me. I was going to ease you into what my life was really like because I..."

The unspoken words hung in the space between them.

Danielle was breaking apart. She'd shattered them both by making assumptions. "Denny." She stood and wiped her eyes with the back of her hands.

He tossed the pillow back on the couch and kept his eyes on it. Softly, he said, "I've been accused of a lot of things. Cheating is a new one for me. I think you should leave."

"I owe you a huge apology."

"I ain't ready for it tonight. Go on now." He still wouldn't look at her.

She felt like she was falling. Like she was being sucked into a hole in the floor and scrabbling her nails for purchase on thin laminate that was getting pulled down with her. She closed her eyes as the pain of what she'd done burst through her chest. How stupid had she been to let a misunderstanding do this to them? She deserved this burning that spread through her limbs and left a numb sensation in their wake. "Okay."

I'm sorry. The words sat right at the tip of her tongue. She wanted to say them so bad, but he'd told her not to. He deserved those words from her, but he wasn't ready to forgive her. She understood, but it didn't make it hurt less. Gritting her teeth, she turned for the door and opened it just wide enough for her to get through.

Tagan stood at the bottom of the porch stairs. In fact, the entire group seemed to be there, milling around in the shadows. Someone had turned strings of holiday lights on, illuminating the dirt road and the dilapidated trailers that lined it.

Heat filled her cheeks. "I guess the walls are pretty thin around here."

"We heard," Tagan said, arching a dark eyebrow.

His bright blue eyes studied her in silence until she was nice and uncomfortable under the scrutiny. She probably had mascara all over her face and looked like a sniffling zombie.

"Denison will help you. I can spare him for a week."

"I don't think he wants that."

"He doesn't have a choice. It's my decision, and what I say goes around here. Anything past a week, we can't help you."

She'd have to mull this over tonight because she definitely wasn't sure she still wanted to do this. The job felt very small in light of everything now. But maybe, just maybe, she could make it up to Denison if he would let her.

Tagan sidled past her and disappeared inside Denison's house. The boys wandered off, talking low, but Skyler and Brooke waited for her to climb down the steps, then flanked her and walked her to the jeep.

"I know you're thinking about leaving," Brooke murmured, "but I think you should stay. If you have a running problem, I can promise you, it won't fix what's been broken with Denison."

"Denny doesn't want me here. He told me to leave."

A door banged and Danielle jumped, then spun in time to see Denison hop over the railing of his porch and stomp off toward a fence that surrounded the trailer park. He didn't even look at her once before he disappeared into the shadows.

She'd done this. Every ounce of pain she'd been through to get over Denison was on her. And the unimaginable agony she'd caused him made her feel like the dirt between the tread on her jeep. "I messed up really bad."

In the distance, a feral roar echoed off the mountains. Danielle hunched as a flock of birds lifted from the nearest tree and flapped off into the night, as if startled by the terrifying noise. "What was that?"

The other women looked at each other, then Brooke draped her arm over Danielle's shoulders. "You're in the wilderness now, Badger. Better get used to the wild animals."

FIVE

A horrendous booming sound traveled down the side of the RV, rattling the metal home. Danielle shot straight up with a yelp and lurched over the edge of the bed.

"Breakfast is on." A voice that sounded suspiciously like Bruiser's called through the thin wall.

Grumpily, she lunged across the tiny living area and threw open the door.

Bruiser's eyebrows shot up, and he rocked backward on his heels. "Whoa there, Badger. You look like hell just spat you out."

Danielle glared. "You know 'knocking' means on the door, not all along the walls, right?"

Bruiser balanced a plate piled with eggs and bacon in one hand and made a sweeping gesture to the ramshackle homes behind him. "Different rules in the trailer park darlin'. You don't like them, you can park your fancy RV on that side of the fence." He shoved the plate of food at her, then spun and walked away. "We're leaving in half an hour. Oh!" He turned his behemoth shoulders and pulled a wadded up length of fabric from his back pocket. "Wear this."

She caught it mid-air and shook it open as best she could while balancing the plate. It was a soft, black T-shirt that read Ashe Crew in bright pink letters.

"The girls made it for you last night. Apparently, they like you, and their opinions count for a hell of a lot around here."

"Bruiser?" she asked as he turned to walk away again.

"What?"

"Where are we going?"

"Lumberjack Wars. We're all competing. Hurry scurry now. We ain't waitin' on you for long."

"Oh." She stared at his back, which was roughly the width of the broad side of a barn. Okay, Lumberjack Wars.

She ate in haste and grabbed some skinny jeans and hiking boots to go with her shirt. She'd showered in a vacant trailer, 1010, last night, but her hair had dried in snarls thanks to the nightmares that roaring animal had given her. Face washed, teeth brushed, and hair swept into a messy bun, she dressed in her new shirt, then plumped her lips with some pink gloss and lengthened her dark lashes with mascara. Ready for the day, she bolted out the front door of her humble abode.

The Ashe Crew, as they apparently called themselves, were bustling here and there to various trucks like frenzied ants. Her eyes lit on Denison like a paperclip to a magnet. He was loading a giant cooler into the back of an old, beat-up green Bronco.

"Hey!" she called, jogging toward him.

Denison closed the back door and frowned. Right, still mad then. Straightening his shoulders, he hooked a hand on his hip and leaned against his ride. The curl of a tattoo showed under his stretched T-shirt. "Hey yourself. What are you doing?"

She lifted her chin and pulled at her shirt so he could read the lettering. "I'm going to cheer you on."

His eyes narrowed as he read the pink lettering. Or perhaps he was just staring at her tits. Either way was fine with her.

"Shotgun," she said.

"Wait, what? What are you doing?"

She marched past him and threw open the passenger's side door. Brighton was leaning on the front nose of the car with an amused grin.

"Brighton has shotgun."

"Brighton?" she asked. "You mind if I sit by your brother?"

Brighton lifted his hands, and his shoulders shook like he was laughing. He canted his head at Denison and pointed to a black truck Brooke and Tagan were loading.

"No," Denison gritted out. "Shotgun is reserved for people who've earned it." He looped an arm around her waist as she tried to crawl inside the Bronco.

"Don't be ridiculous," she muttered, clutching onto the grab handle and hooking her shoes inside the doorframe. "Nobody's riding with you now, and

I'm not sitting in the back like you are my chauffeur."

"Damn straight you aren't. Go ride with Tagan."

He pulled harder, but she was spry.

"Stop being stubborn!"

He yanked her out of his car and spun her around to face him. His eyes flashed with something that wasn't altogether anger, and she pounced.

"Let me ride with you," she muttered, scrambling for purchase on the dry gravel he was dragging her across. "Or so help me, Denny, I'll kiss you soundly right on the lips, and then where will you be?"

He let her loose and crossed his arms over his chest. "I'll be unaffected."

"I'm irresistible."

He snorted a laugh and tried to hold his frown, but lost it as his lips turned up in a smile. Scrubbing his hands down his face, which he still hadn't shaved, the sexy mountain man, he let off a sigh and let her go. "I think God sent you here to kill me, woman."

She scrambled inside the Bronco and slammed the door, then tossed him a victory grin. She wasn't for sure, because the words were muffled by the car, but she thought he said something along the lines of, "Freaking badger."

When he went to open the driver's side door, she hit the automatic lock button just as he pulled the lever. Oh, he looked so annoyed, but underneath was that hint of a smile she used to breathe for. Heck, from the way her heart was fluttering around in her chest like bat wings, maybe she still breathed for it now.

"You gonna annoy me all day long?" he asked, trying to look severe as he turned the engine.

"I've decide something," she said, ignoring his question. "I'm going to make you forgive me."

"Danielle," he warned.

"No, hear me out. I know I messed up. Bad. But you aren't the only one who got hurt, Denny. The only way I can feel okay about us being friends again is if I make it up to you. So today, I'm going to be your beer wench." She patted her purse and grinned. "Anytime you want a beer, I'm your girl."

He put his hand on the back of her headrest, and she leaned toward him instinctively. Twisting in his seat and backing the car away from his trailer, he said, "Your plan to win my friendship is by getting me beer?"

"Yeah."

He nodded once and pulled in line behind Kellen's truck. "Okay then."

"And I'll also be extra nice to you and cheer the loudest when you are doing lumberjack stuff."

Denison shot her a glance and lowered his eyes to the writing on her chest again, then back to the road in front of them. "I like that shirt on you."

"Brooke and Skyler made it for me. Where did you get the name Ashe Crew?"

This was where Denison had always clammed up in the past. Anything personal made him uncomfortable, but he shrugged his shoulders and explained, "That name has been around a long time, and not just for this crew we have assembled now. It's been a name that's been carried on through generations."

"Of lumberjacks?"

"Sure."

"And are there other crews of lumberjacks?"

"Yeah, two others that live in these mountains. The Gray Backs are a crew like ours who work a jobsite up the road, and the Boarlanders are a crew of cutters. They cut the trees, and we haul them away to the sawmill in Saratoga or to log buyers."

Until now, she hadn't thought about the impact on the environment—on the ecosystem here. Animals depended on those trees for homes and for food, but Denison and his crew were chopping them down and selling off the forest.

"You have your judgey face on," he accused.

"Not judging, just thinking."

"We re-plant as we go."

"You do?" Huh.

"You're here for the beetle infestation, to study it, right? Well, right now, the land here is just dry, dead tinder waiting for a spark. And it won't be one of those controlled forest fires that help the forest to regrow. It'll be an inferno when it burns. Damon Daye owns most of this land up here. He and his family have been buying it up for generations, and it's he who hired the crews to come manage the territory. He isn't trying to hurt this place by taking the trees. He's trying to salvage it."

"My my, Denison Donovan Beck. You have a land lovin', tree huggin' mountain man inside of you." It was sexy when he talked about the woods like this. Like he cared.

Her eyes drifted to the inky tendril that showed

just under the sleeve of his shirt. "The tattoo is new." She lifted up the edge of his sleeve, but he shrugged away.

"It's not new. I got it the year you left."

"What is it?" Besides sexy. All she'd been able to make out were intricate tribal shapes that didn't form anything she could make any sense of.

"Maybe if you earn my forgiveness, I'll tell you."

There was no *if*, only *when*. She'd stayed awake late into the night going over the things she'd done wrong and how she could've handled it differently. The only way she could forgive herself was to earn his trust and be the friend he deserved.

She tossed him a saucy look. "Someday you'll show me yours, and then I'll show you mine."

It had been a tease, but when she looked over at him, the smile had dipped from his face, and his smoldering eyes raked down her body, drawing a delicious tremor up her spine. Warmth pooled between her legs when he slid his hand to her thigh and gripped it.

"You'll show me your ink first, little badger," he said low, attention back on the road.

"Want to make a bet?" she asked.

"Name the terms."

"First person to cave has to do whatever the other one wants."

Denison narrowed his eyes on the road. "Deal." He slammed on the brakes and jerked the wheel. Danielle held onto the grab handle for dear life as he maneuvered through the trees. Tagan didn't even slow as he passed them to follow Kellen's truck as Brooke waved out the window with a curious smile.

Away from the road, Denison pulled to a stop and threw the car into park.

"What are you—"

He reached under the seat and slammed his chair back, then grabbed her waist and pulled her over onto his lap like she weighed nothing.

Oh.

He leaned up and his lips crashed onto hers with such force, she whimpered at the sheer shock of it. He wasn't the soft Denny she remembered. This Denny was different. Everything she remembered was null and void now as he parted her lips and plunged his tongue against hers. But for as different as he seemed, this somehow felt like home. Right here, straddling his lap as his hands ran over her back and gripped her tighter. Nothing had come close to this in the years she'd tried to move on.

When her breasts heaved, they brushed his chest. He sucked her bottom lip and rattled a hungry sound from deep within his throat, drawing a gasp from her. The Denny she'd known had been reserved and careful when they were together like this. Denny now was half-feral and fully sexy.

She rolled her hips against his thick erection that pressed against his pants. He groaned and gripped her hair, angling her neck. He flicked his tongue against the tripping pulse at the base of her throat as she rocked against him again.

His hand slid under her shirt, up her ribs, and unsnapped her bra in back with a fucking professional flick of his fingers. He cupped her breast, and she cried out and arched against his hand. God, what that man could do to her body with a touch.

"You want more?"

"More. Please more," she panted out.

He pressed his mouth over her breast, the thin material of the T-shirt the only thing between her oversensitive skin and his lips. He blew air until her nipple drew up tight. His tongue lapped until the shirt was wet and she was just about undone. The man was going to make her come without ever touching between her legs. Desperate for more, she pulled his hand and guided him to the top button of her jeans.

He eased back, then whispered softly in her ear. "You're a needy little badger, aren't you?" Plucking gently, he pulled her earlobe into his mouth and grazed his teeth against it.

The button of her jeans popped open under his steady fingers, and the rip of the zipper filled the Bronco. When he slid his hand under her panties and cupped her sex, she bucked helplessly against him.

He smiled and nibbled her bottom lip again. "You were always good at getting wet for me."

When he slid his finger into her slick opening, he brushed her clit like he knew the exact spot that would drive her mad with want.

"Oh!" she cried out. "Denny, please."

"Fuck yes, more of that. Tell me what you want."

He pulled his finger out slowly, then added another before he pressed into her again. Her belly quivered with intense pleasure. Leaning forward, she tasted his lips and matched her pace with his hand. He relaxed against the seat and took his time bringing her to climax. She hadn't been able to finish with anyone since him.

He'd been her first.

Her best.

He should've been her only.

And right when she was about to tip over the edge, he stilled, just shy of touching her clit again. His eyes grew serious as he held her gaze. "Just friends doesn't work for me. You want my forgiveness? You give me another shot. A real one this time where you don't run when you get scared. Now show me that tattoo, and I'll let you fuck my hand."

Her thoughts raced with what she was considering. If she did this, if she gave in, there was no more going back. Oh, she knew what he was saying. He was laying claim to her heart, right here in the middle of the woods, and asking her to take a leap of faith with him.

If she said no, she wouldn't be able to go back to her life and not be affected by how intense her feelings still were with him. Saying no wasn't an option anymore. Not when it would hurt so badly again.

"I won't run, if you let me in." Negotiations, oh

yes. She was good at haggling.

"Done. You might not like what you find out, though."

She leveled him with her gaze and cupped his cheeks. Lowering her voice and rocking against his hand, she said, "I won't run."

With a deep, steadying breath, she lifted her shirt over her head and shrugged out of her loose bra. Then she turned and showed him the tiny arrow tattoo on the side of her ribcage. "No matter how far an arrow is drawn back, it always shoots forward again."

He dragged his gaze from the tiny mark with a smile of triumph. He was beautiful like this, confident and happy, staring at her like he'd never seen another so alluring. He pressed his finger into her again, but she shook her head.

"I want all of you now."

He hesitated, and she thought he would reject her. Embarrassed at putting herself out there like this, she murmured, "I'm on birth control if that's what you're worried about."

"That's not... I'm worried about bonding to you even more, and then you leaving again."

She frowned and stroked the shadow-colored stubble on his jaw. "You're already bonded to me, Denny. And I'm not going anywhere. I made a mistake before."

He dropped his eyes to the door handle and for a moment, he looked lost.

"Denny," she whispered, pulling his face back to hers. Her pulse hammered as she realized her feelings for him hadn't diminished at all, no matter how hard she'd tried to snuff him from her heart. "I'm sorry." Sorrier than he would ever know.

He pulled her nipple into his mouth and dragged his tongue against it until it tingled. When he eased back again, he looked surer of himself, as if he'd made up his mind. Kicking open the door with his heavy work boot, he slipped from the car. When he turned back to her, he was unbuttoning his pants, and she smiled.

"Say it. Say you forgive me."

"You haven't bought me a single beer," he teased as he eased his long, thick cock from his briefs.

Her heart thrummed erratically against her sternum as she watched him stroke himself from the base to the tip. It was red and swollen, ready for her, and she shimmied out of her jeans as fast as she could peel the danged things off.

"I like that you're smooth," he whispered reverently. Gripping the backs of her knees, he pulled her legs until her hips rested on the edge of the seat. He knelt down between her thighs and stared at her sex. "I like being able to see all of you."

He eased her back and dragged his tongue along her slick seam. Her shoulders shook with the tremor that blasted up her spine, and she arched her head back and closed her eyes. The sensation of his whiskers against her skin was nothing shy of orgasmic. His tongue lapped at her, three languid strokes, then he stood and leaned into the Bronco, over her body, and trailed soft kisses up her bare stomach.

When he came to her tattoo, he paused, then kissed it. "You're mine, Danielle." His voice was pitched low and had a gravelly quality she'd never heard before.

She dragged her fingernails across his shoulders and sighed at the happiness that filled her. "You're mine too, Denny. I think you always have been."

He rattled off a low growl and plunged his shaft

into her, filling and stretching her. He felt so good, so familiar, as if they were meant to be here, connected. As if they were better when they were together.

He opened his eyes just before his lips collided with hers, and she saw it. Something hidden beneath the surface. Something churning and silver and incomprehensible. He thrust into her again, and she bowed against him and clawed his back. She didn't care if she hurt his skin. She wanted him to feel her here. To be marked by what they were doing in these quiet woods. This wasn't just making love. She felt it to her bones. This was more. Denison was tethering her to him with every stroke.

He bucked harder, pulling her tightly against his chest as his teeth grazed her skin. She yelled out his name as she detonated around him, and he froze and threw his head back. The muscles in his neck strained before he brought his cool, silvery gaze back to her. It wasn't a trick of the lighting this time—she knew for sure. Denny was different, and those eyes... He was hiding something scary inside of him. She hadn't a guess what, but right now as he filled her with pulsing, hot jets, filled her until she overflowed and wetness trickled between her thighs, she didn't care that he kept secrets.

Someday, she was going to prove she was worth sharing them with.

He slammed into her three more times as his cock swelled and emptied completely. Spent, he nuzzled her neck and stroked her hair until their breathing slowed and their pounding heartbeats synchronized at a much slower pace.

"I've missed you," he said so softly she almost didn't hear it.

She smiled at the ceiling of the Bronco and ran her fingers through his hair, her heart full as a future with the man she'd always loved stretched on and on before her. "I've missed you, too."

SIX

Danielle moved to open the car door, but Denison reached over her lap and pulled it closed again. When she turned to ask him what he thought he was doing, he cupped the back of her neck and pulled her closer. Hesitating half a beat, he dropped his gaze to her lips, then kissed her. It wasn't one of those powerful lip-locks that tried to make up for lost time, but a sweet one with a gentle pluck of her bottom lip before he pulled away with a soft smacking sound that made her insides feel like they were glowing.

"I'm sorry if I pushed us too far earlier. I was

going to stop when you showed me your tattoo, but I let things get a little out of hand."

She nibbled his bottom lip, then glared. "Are you done apologizing for sleeping with me?"

"It wasn't just sleeping together. Not to me. It was—"

The window popped three times, scaring the glow right out of her. Bruiser stood leaned against the Bronco, grinning at her through the glass. "Took y'all long enough."

Startled, Danielle clutched her chest, as if it would keep her heart from escaping, and shoved the door open. Hiding her burning cheeks, she slung her purse strap across her torso and made her way toward Brooke and Skyler.

Looking at paperwork, the others stood in a loose half-circle around the open tailgate of Kellen's truck. The parking lot was nothing more than an open field full of calf-length waving grass and wild flowers.

Brooke waved from the other side of a lower, marshy area that was still holding water from the recent rains. As Danielle prepared to jump over the tiny creek, her feet flipped out from under her and before she knew it, she was thrown over Denison's shoulder like a sack of cat food. She yelped when his big palm smacked her bum soundly. He hopped over the water like she weighed nothing and let out a booming laugh as she pummeled his butt with her closed fist.

"Denison Donavan Beck!"

"Oh, he got the full name, boys. Denison's in trouble!" Bruiser called as he hopped over the tiny stream behind then.

Danielle arched her back and glared at him, but the jokester only chuckled harder.

Denny set her down so fast she gasped, but he didn't miss a step. Grabbing her hand, he pulled her against his side, then draped his arm around her shoulders and called behind him, "If she wasn't getting me in trouble, I'd be worried she was sick or something."

"Har, har," she muttered, but she couldn't help the grin that was cracking her face wide open. She'd been afraid Denison would act like there wasn't something simmering between them in front of his friends, but nope. Apparently, Denison was making their budding relationship status public.

His utterly comfortable behavior added another layer of seriousness to the naked party they'd had in the Bronco earlier. He wasn't just sleeping with her. He still cared for her enough to make his feelings obvious in front of the people who meant the most to him.

A familiar warmth flooded her veins and made her go all gooey as she remembered how he used to make her feel when they were together. He'd never acted ashamed of being with her. His obvious pride at her being on his arm had always made her feel coveted, and it seemed that part of their relationship hadn't changed.

Drew sniffed her hair as Denison led her past and murmured, "Mmm, pheromones."

A low growl emanated from Denison, and Drew backed off.

Could he smell what they'd done? Heat flared hotter in her cheeks.

"Leave them alone," Brooke said as she made room between her and Skyler where they were leaning against the oversize white pickup.

Denison squeezed her hand and kissed the side of her head where he allowed his lips to linger. When he pulled away, he said, "I'm in the first event, but my heat doesn't start for another forty-five minutes. We're going to plan who is going to do what events and go sign up. You can stay here or go see what they have going on over there." He pointed to a group of tents and vendors.

She didn't want to stand around and take Denison's attention off what Tagan was talking low to the others about, so she jerked her chin at Brooke and Skyler and scrunched her nose, a little nervous they'd reject what she was about to propose. "Are you hungry?"

"Starving," Skyler said as she pulled her dark hair into a high ponytail. "I'm in an event later today, and I don't want to eat too close to it. Let's find some grub."

"I'm down for finding food," Brooke said. "I skipped breakfast."

"Brooke," Tagan admonished, suddenly looking up from the paperwork stacked on the tailgate.

"It was too early," Brooke explained. "If I eat that early, I'll feel sick all day."

Tagan angled his head and gave Brooke a worried frown before returning to a conversation about something called a hot saw.

"You want me to grab something for you?" Danielle asked Denison, who was still lingering beside her instead of joining his crew.

"Yeah, just get me whatever you think sounds good. Here." He reached in the back pocket of his jeans and pulled out his wallet.

"No! Beer wench today," she said. "Remember?"

A slow smile crept across his face, exposing a dimple in his left cheek. She fought the urge to touch it. He licked his bottom lip and nodded. "Okay. If you're paying, get me double." He laughed and ducked out of swatting range. Quick as a snake, he leaned in and pecked her on the forehead, then jogged over and joined his crew at the back of the truck.

Danielle giggled—giggled! Like a teen with a crush and not a twenty-four-year-old woman who was supposed to be keeping her cool about all of this. Danielle followed Brooke and Skyler toward the first tent, but looked back because she couldn't help herself. Denison was watching her leave, and when she smiled, he winked at her and gave her a slow-simmering grin that just about locked her knees.

That man was a charmer and a mystery, but most of all, Denny was going to wreak havoc on her hormones.

She jogged and caught up to the girls, but when she did, Brooke lifted her hair and studied the back of her neck.

"What are you doing?" Danielle asked, locking her legs and halting.

"Checking for a bite mark," Brooke said nonchalantly.

Okay. "Like a vampire bite mark?" She hadn't exactly believed in things-that-go-bump-in-the-night before now, but something was definitely different with Denison. His changing eyes were supernatural for sure. They were like two damned mood rings right on his face, telling her when he was pissed or turned on.

Skyler rocked back on her heels and laughed. "No vampires around here." She frowned. "At least, not that we know of." She turned to Brooke and shook her head as she shoved her hands in the pockets of her jeans. "He wouldn't bite her. Danielle's human—"

"Skyler!" Brooke admonished. Her eyes went

round and serious, and her voice changed. Deepened as if her words held weight. "That's enough. Good grief, do we have to censor you *and* Kellen now?"

"Well, blame that on him. He talks about whatever he likes all the time, and I get used to it. Maybe you should drag us to town more often. Living in the Asheland bubble ain't doin' us any favors." Skyler crossed her arms in front of her chest with a pouty frown.

"Why would Denison bite me?" Danielle asked. "I'm assuming it isn't just for kink."

"All the boys are biters. Forget I said anything," Brooke muttered and began walking again.

"Are you two like Denison?" Danielle tested.

"Like Denison how?" Skyler asked, sounding too innocent.

Well, crap, she hadn't figured out a guess yet. "Zombies?"

Brooke snorted and kept her face carefully hidden behind her blond locks.

"Yeti?"

Now Skyler was laughing, too.

"Give me a hint," Danielle pleaded. "All I've got are glowing eyes and growling... Oh, werewolf!"

"No, and stop guessing," Brooke said with a little worried moue to her glossed lips. "*If* there was anything different about Denison and *if* he decided he wanted you to know, he would tell you when he was good and ready."

Danielle narrowed her eyes and sighed. "Fine." It was just like last time she'd lived here when she was the odd woman out. Everyone was in on the secret, but nobody trusted her enough to let her in. It stung and made her realize she wasn't part of this trio of friends. She was just a tagalong.

"I'm going to go get Denison some food before his event. I'll see you later."

She turned to leave, but Brooke hugged her from behind, arms squeezing Danielle's collar bones. "I know how it feels," she whispered. "Feeling like everyone knows but you. You have to be patient, though. It's not my place, or Skyler's place, to spill secrets that aren't ours."

Danielle's eyes burned with emotion, and she held still as Brooke hugged her tighter.

"I had to wait, and Skyler went through hell finding her way into the Ashe Crew, too," Brooke explained. "You're Denison's girl, and if it were up to me, you'd already know how much you belong to us. It's not up to me, though. I'll tell you something I haven't told anyone but Tagan, so you'll know you have my trust."

Skyler stepped in front of Danielle with a worried look in her bright green eyes.

Danielle could feel Brooke smile against her ear. "I'm pregnant."

Skyler's eyebrows drew up, and her eyes rimmed with tears. "Already?"

Danielle didn't understand the dynamics here. Had Brooke and Tagan been trying for a baby for a long time? Had they suffered a loss?

Brooke pulled her and Skyler into a hug. "It's hard for our kind to have babies," she whispered so low Danielle almost missed it. "It's why I've been having a hard time eating. I feel sick all the time, and we haven't told the boys, so please don't say anything. We wanted to make sure the baby is okay before we get everyone worked up."

"The crew is going to lose their shit," Skyler murmured. A slow smile stretched her lips. "We're gonna have a baby." The first tear slipped down Skyler's cheek, and Danielle thumbed it away, then hugged them both closer.

She didn't understand why it was hard for Brooke and Tagan to have a baby, or why Skyler worded it like the Ashe crew was having a child instead of just Brooke, or why a bunch of foul-mouthed, beer-guzzling, caveman trailer boys would care one way or the other about a baby, but she knew one thing—these were good people. People who cared deeply for one another and who were trying to let her in as much as they could. She wanted to be a part of this. She wanted to be accepted by Denison's friends and become someone they could depend on, like they obviously depended on each other.

"Okay, okay," Danielle said, giving them one last squeeze. "Let's go feed this baby."

****

The last half hour had been spent gathering food. Two rows of stands sat in a fog of savory scents that ranged from sausage to fresh fried pork rinds to hand-dipped corn dogs to gourmet pizza pies. Brooke had already inhaled a pair of three-cheese and meatball sandwiches by the time they made their way toward several sixty-foot poles towering along the outer edge of the crowded fairgrounds.

Danielle watched in horror as eight men ran up the poles with spiked shoes and a single belt thrown around the log. "They don't have safety harnesses," she said as her acute fear of heights threatened to freeze her into place.

"They don't need them," Skyler said, handing a bartender, who was set up right alongside the event, a couple of dollars. "This is an easy one for them, and that leather strap keeps them safe enough."

"Safe enough," Danielle repeated as she imagined Denison making it to the very top and plummeting to his death.

Out of nowhere, a man ran into her. "Excuse me," he apologized, steadying her with his hands on her upper arms.

Her plate of food wobbled, but she righted it. "It's fine. Sorry, I wasn't watching where I was going."

Tall enough to look down at her, the man was lanky, but not whiplash thin, with dark hair gone gray at the temples. His words had been polite enough, but his hazel eyes were lifeless and cold. A chill ran up her back as she jerked out of his grasp.

The man lifted his chin and looked down his nose at her, then slid his eyes to Brooke and Skyler before an empty smile stretched his thin lips. His eyes narrowed as he said, "Sorry for disturbing you, ladies. You all have a nice day now." His deep voice sounded so familiar.

Danielle watched him go with a strange feeling in her gut. Like déjà vu, or as if she'd lived this exact moment before.

"He was weird," Brooke said low. "You okay?"

"Yeah," Danielle muttered, shaking off the tingly feeling that had raised the fine hairs on the back of her neck. "I'm fine."

Brooke turned toward the bartender and ordered a cold one for Tagan. Danielle rubbed the back of her neck and watched the stranger leave. He looked back at her once before he stepped behind a tent and out of sight.

"Hey," a passing man said, pointing to Danielle. "I know you."

She dragged her attention away from where the man had disappeared, and her stomach dipped to her toes. It was that asshole, Matt, from Sammy's bar.

"Uh, no you don't," she said, her mood plummeting.

Maybe if she just ignored him...

Turning, she pointed to a cooler of non-alcoholic beverages and asked the bartender, "Can I get one of those lime-flavored electrolyte drinks?"

Skyler was glaring at Matt, while Brooke gave her a knowing smile and asked, "What, no beer for Denison before the event?"

"Hell no. He needs to keep his head." What a terrible beer wench she made. She paid for the drink as fast as her shaking hands could manage and tried to hightail it out of there before Matt the Horny Brat reached her.

Too late.

"I knew it. You're the hot chick from the bar. Damn, girl. You look even better in broad daylight."

"I'm surprised you even remember me." *Ratfincked whiskey-breathing butt-groper.* "We're running late, so have a nice life." She grabbed Skyler's arm and hurried behind Brooke toward the crowd waiting below the poles.

"Wait," Matt said, pulling her shoulder and stopping her escape. "We're going to the same place." He jerked his chin to an event sign that read *90' Climb.* "I'll walk you."

"She doesn't need you to walk her, Gray Back,"

Skyler said. Her eyes had gone deadly as she stared up at the man. "Can you not read her shirt?"

He was six-feet-three and had nearly a foot on Skyler, but she didn't look intimidated at all. Skyler gave him a humorless smile and said, "Now, kindly fuck off."

Danielle snorted a laugh and tried to cover it with a cough. Dear goodness, it was awesome to watch tiny Skyler face off with the handsy Sasquatch.

Danielle sidled by Skyler, gave him a little wave, and caught up with Brooke. The green drink sloshed in its plastic container and was cold against her hand, but before she knew what happened, it was slapped out of her palm and lay in the shadows of a make-shift alleyway between two tents.

"I apologize," Matt said from right beside her. "Let me get that. My silly hand just does what it wants sometimes."

Gads, he was fast. He'd been ten paces behind her, then right there in no time at all. Anger flared up the back of Danielle's neck as she rushed to retrieve the drink.

Matt bent down, too, and snatched it from under her grasp. "Too slow," he murmured, his face only inches from hers. "Do you know what you smell like from here?"

"Denison," she gritted out.

"Yeah, that's right, baby. You smell like an Ashe Crew whore."

Fury, red and hot, blasted up her arm. She drew back and slapped him hard. "Don't you talk to me like that. I'm with Denison. I'm not anyone's whore."

Matt's blazing blue eyes filled with hatred, and he leaned forward and gripped her hair, then yanked her to him and kissed her so hard she tasted iron. Danielle struggled against his impossible grip. Where were Skyler and Brooke? She searched for them out of her peripheral vision, but they seemed to be blocked out of the alleyway by a trio of equally big men with Gray Back Crew T-shirts on. Shit.

Matt released her throbbing lip and growled out, "You should've picked a real man to fuck you first. Now you'll never know better."

Something big and powerful launched her backward, and when she sat up, Matt wasn't taunting her anymore. He was locked up, absorbing blow after blow from Brighton. Brighton?

Strong arms picked her up and turned her out of

the alley. It was Bruiser, and Drew was waiting with his arms crossed, watching Brighton beat the stuffing out of Matt. The giant was getting in a punch here and there, but Brighton was lethal and didn't even react to the crushing blows Matt snuck in.

Holy shit, he was fast.

"Let's get you out of here," Bruiser said. "Brighton."

Just like that, Brighton pushed Matt into a couple of Gray Backs and followed her out of the alley. They led her through a maze of vendors, Bruiser's hands never straying from the upper part of her arm. When they came to an abandoned tent with a few scattered tables, Brighton took her hand and led her to the farthest one. Easing her down into a plastic chair, he jerked his head to the others and Bruiser and Drew backed off.

"Brighton, Skyler and Brooke were back there," she wheezed out, panicked.

He shook his head and stripped his shirt off, then looked behind him as if he were making sure they weren't being followed. "They're okay." His voice wasn't a voice at all, but a barely audible whisper of air. "Tagan and Haydan have them."

Her throbbing lip took a backseat to her shock. "You can talk?"

He pointed to a long, red mark where his short beard didn't grow whiskers on his neck. "No," he rasped out, voiceless.

She didn't understand. "Is that a scar? Did someone do this to you?"

She could see him close down on her. The emotion in his emerald green eyes went dead. He inhaled deeply and whispered, "Denison can't see you like this. He'll kill them."

Brighton dabbed the side of her lip, and when he pulled his shirt away, it was smeared with crimson. Son of a mother fluffin' biscuit eater. Matt, that dick-faced weasel-turd had made her bleed with his uninvited kiss.

Brighton stared at her lip with a frown, then turned to Drew, who jogged over. He pulled at her lip and leaned in close, studying the cut. "He didn't get her deep enough. She won't Turn."

Brighton huffed out a relieved-sounding sigh and leaned his head back, then stared at her with his dark eyebrows arched high.

Slowly, she asked, "Turn me into what?"

All Brighton whispered before he pulled his shirt on and dragged her back out of the tent was, "A Gray Back."

SEVEN

Brighton could talk. Okay, he couldn't make sound, but he could communicate, and as far as Danielle could remember, he'd never whispered to her before. And right now, he was guiding her through the crowd with his hand protectively on her lower back with Bruiser and Drew flanking them.

"Brighton?"

He cast her a quick glance.

"How did you know to come find us?"

He leaned in close so she could hear the brush of air that formed his words. "You called for Denison. He was too far away."

She hadn't actually called for Denison. She'd said his name, at normal volume, to Matt, and somehow Brighton and the boys had heard her. Danielle's curiosity was growing by the minute.

It was apparent almost immediately why Denison hadn't been involved in the Ashe Crew's little rescue mission. The 90' Climb had begun, and Danielle watched in awe as he propelled himself upward on powerful legs. He made it look easy and graceful, as if he were running on the ground instead up straight up into the sky. His arms flexed each time he pulled the strip of leather up around the pole to gain more traction. Holy hell balls, she'd known Denison was hot, but the man had learned many a talent in the time she'd been away.

"He is the best one for this event," Drew said low. "He's the one who usually runs cable up the pole to create our skylines at the different job sites we've worked. Heights don't get to any of us, and we're comfortable in trees, but Denison is the fastest on time."

Two other men reached the top near Denison, but he was first. One of the competitors wore a T-shirt like Matt that read *Gray Back Crew*, and the other said *Boarlander Crew*. The other five competitors were way behind and looked clumsy compared to the three men at the top.

Danielle clutched the drink she'd bought and debated whether to watch Denison climb down. He seemed completely comfortable in his element, though, and it was hard to take her eyes off him. He was smiling, as if he was enjoying himself, and a knot of tension slid from her shoulders.

Matt wasn't going to ruin today.

"Are you okay?" Brooke asked, fighting the crowd to get to her. Skyler, Tagan, and Haydan followed close behind.

"I'm fine," Danielle assured them. "Just mad that guy won't take a hint."

"He won't mess with you anymore," Tagan said in a quiet voice.

Something about the way he said it made her believe him. Tagan seemed like the most reserved out of the bunch, but he had that look sometimes that said he was a brawler when he had to be. Like Brighton.

Denison said a few words to a man with clipboard, then looked out over the crowd until he saw her. With a grin, he made his way through the onlookers, then swept her up into a back-cracking hug. With a quick spin, he searched her face, but his smile dropped when his eyes landed on her lip.

He set her down immediately and kissed her gently where it hurt the most. "You're bleeding." He kissed her again, and warmth spread from the tiny cut through her lip. It made it feel numb and tingly. Easing back, he asked, "What happened?"

"Nothing you need to worry about," Tagan said gruffly.

Denison narrowed his eyes at his friend and froze. He looked to his brother, then behind him, where a group of Gray Backs were gathered. Matt was with them.

Time for a shift in conversation. "I brought you a drink." Danielle shoved the sports drink in his hand. "I was afraid to get you beer because I thought it would inhibit you, but clearly you can handle yourself just fine," she rambled. "I dropped all of our food, though. You can make bad beer wench jokes now."

Denny looked at her and blinked slowly. "Stop. Who did that to your face? Did someone hit you?"

"No, it was nothing like that."

Over Denison's shoulder, Skyler looked green in the face. Okay, no one was speaking up to get her out of this, and something heavy was settling over her chest, like static from a lightning storm. The air even smelled different now. She couldn't put her finger on what it was exactly. A little woodsy with undercurrents of animal.

"Denison," Tagan said, stepping in front of him and blocking him off from Danielle's view. "I forbid you going after him. We took care of it, Brighton avenged your mate, the girls are safe, and we can't afford a war. Keep it to the competition."

"Tagan," Denison said in a helpless, choked voice.

The sound tore at Danielle's heart, and she pushed around Tagan's wide shoulders.

Denison's eyes were blazing a frosty silvery-white. "Not here, Denny," she said, resting her hands on his chest. "I'm okay." Something tapped on her shoulder, and when she looked over, Brighton was handing her a pair of sunglasses.

The crew surged forward, surrounding them as she slid the glasses over his eyes to shield them from the crowd.

She tried to smile, but her lip trembled. Cupping

his cheeks, she whispered, "I swear I'm okay."

Denison leaned forward until his forehead rested on hers. "Tell me what happened quick."

"He kissed me. I hated it. He was trying to get to you. That's all." She'd leave out the whore comment and hope Denny didn't ever catch wind of it. He didn't seem the type to let something like that go.

He pulled her lip gently down with his thumb. She couldn't see his expression anymore behind the glasses, but he looked at the tiny wound for what felt like minutes. "Not deep enough," he murmured. "You're hungry. I need to feed you." His voice had taken on a dreamy quality.

Her stomach was growling. Her corndog sat on the grass where she'd dropped it when Matt had kiss-attacked her. Uninvited face molestation plus a ruined hand-battered corndog equaled Matt getting a serious kick in the gonads next time she saw him.

****

Denison was going to bleed that Gray Back slowly. He couldn't do it today because Tagan, his alpha, had ordered him not to, but someday Matt was going to feel deep pain and regret for hurting Danielle.

He turned and glared at Matt across the crowd. The asshole had the balls to toss him a taunting grin, but it was hard to take it seriously behind the bruising and the broken nose that his shifter healing was struggling to fix. Brighton must've got him good. He wished it was him to avenge Danielle's treatment, but if he couldn't, his twin was second best at settling down his inner bear. God, his animal was roaring for blood. Everything was bathed in shades of red. Everything except for Danielle, who kept pulling his face back to her. The only red on her was the tiny smear at the corner of her mouth Denison wanted to clean off with his tongue. He gave in once more, thinking it would calm his bear, and kissed it clean. Danielle gave off the most delicious little moan as he sucked her lip, and he hoped that touching her affected her like it did shifters. Warmth spreading through her limbs, calming her from the inside out. That's why he had to stay near the Ashe Crew. Their presence calmed the raging animal inside of him better than a tranquilizer. And they knew it, too. Bruiser's hand had been on his shoulder the entire time since he'd learned Matt had gone after Danielle. That, Tagan's order, and Danielle's pleading eyes kept him from lunging over the crowd of unknowing humans and ripping Matt's throat out through his stomach.

If Danielle knew what he really was, what he was really capable of, she'd run away and never come back.

Matt had come way too close to Turning her into a bear shifter. If he would've gone deeper, bit her harder, she would've been a Gray Back by law. He repressed a shudder at the thought. War would've been unavoidable then.

If she was a born bear shifter, this could've been avoided. He could've claimed her when they were together in the Bronco earlier, and Matt wouldn't have any right to mess with her. As it stood, he didn't want this life for her. Didn't want to Turn her for his own happiness. Being a bear was awful and painful at times. It would mean hiding what was inside of her for the rest of her life. Brooke struggled with it still, and she'd been Turned by a man she loved. Denison didn't know if Danielle was quite there yet. His bear had chosen her years ago, and when she'd left, he'd had to accept that he would be mate-less forever. But now she was back, and he couldn't rush this. And if she didn't want the bear inside of her and didn't fully understand what she'd be giving up—namely, her humanity—he was going to make damned sure she was never touched by the tooth of a shifter. Not even his own. Not even to claim her and bond her to him completely.

He and Brighton knew the dangers of being different from humans. They'd paid in agony for that knowledge. Danielle couldn't ever know that fear.

Matt had gotten too close to Turning her though, and it dumped panic into his system. He could've so easily bitten into her muscle, been more thorough, ruined her life. Ruined Denison's shot at happiness with the woman he still loved more than anything.

He didn't know what he was going to do, but one thing was for sure. He had to keep her away from the Gray Backs and the Boarlanders until she decided for herself if she wanted this life or not.

What if she ran? No. She was different now. He pulled her against his chest and rested his chin on top of her head. She was stronger now. Matt hurt her, but she still showed up here, trying to play it off like no big deal to protect Denison from doing something stupid in a crowd full of humans. And she didn't even know what he was.

Maybe she could handle all of his secrets.

Not now, but someday.

"Come on. There's not much time between events, and Tagan is up next." He needed to take care of her in some way to soothe the rampaging animal inside of him, and feeding her was all he could do right now. Tonight, he was going to take her home and adore her body. Not in some quickie passion-fuck like he'd pushed in the Bronco. But better, slower, like she deserved. He inhaled her scent—fruit shampoo, soap, blood, and the lingering bitter smell of fear. That last trace threatened to buckle him and force a Change, but he couldn't lose it here.

As if she could read the turmoil flooding him, she stood on tiptoes and kissed him. Giving into his need for her, he pulled her closer and slid his tongue past the seam of her lips to taste her. God, his mate was perfect.

His mate? Hell yeah. She had been for years, and this time he was going to do this right. He was going to share more of himself and hope she stayed around for the ugly parts.

History said he wasn't good enough to keep her,

but this time he was going to show her exactly how important—no, pivotal—she was in his life.

He squeezed her tiny hand in his, wrapping his fingers all the way around. He clapped Brighton on the back in a silent "thank you" for being there for his mate when he wasn't able. He owed his brother, big time.

Most of the crew followed Tagan toward the Standing Block Chop, but Denison pulled Danielle toward the rows of concession stands. And when his mate was satisfied with food, and they both had a cold beer in hand, he draped his arm around her waist and reveled in the fact that she'd come back to him. She'd chosen him, not Matt, or some guy she'd met after she'd left. She'd come back because of that job, but it was a cover. He knew in his gut she'd really come back because she still felt something for Denison. She'd thought about him through the years and had been brave enough to face her fears of his rejection and come back. He felt like the luckiest man in the world with her laughing beside him as they watched Tagan dominate in his event and while she cheered with him as they watched Skyler take second in the Women's Boom Run across a bunch of logs connected together in the nearby lake.

As the day wore on, his bear settled under Danielle's constant touch. She seemed as thirsty for his skin as he was for hers. Her smiles were constant, and only for him and the Ashe Crew. She looked so damned sexy in the shirt that proclaimed she was part of his team. She laughed and talked to his friends like they were family, and it made him even more devoted to her.

She'd always been a nature nerd and big into her books on trees and plants, but she'd never been awkward like she'd said. The Crew had always liked her.

Now, she was a spitfire and didn't take shit from any of them without dishing it back. Denison didn't have to defend her or take up for her or soothe her hurt feelings. She just grinned at their insults, then handed them back like she'd always been a part of this group of sailor-mouthed, rough-talkin' men.

As the sun set low in the sky and the Ashe Crew all sat on the bank of the lake passing around a giant bowl of fruit salad Skyler had brought in one of the coolers, Denison looked around and thought his life couldn't possibly get better than it was right now.

Danielle looked so happy to be here, nestled under the crook of his arm as she asked questions about the Boarlanders, Gray Backs, and the different machines up on the job site. She seemed so worried about the dangers of being a lumberjack.

This was the first time today where they had an hour in between events. He'd done a couple of the chopping events and a log throwing one with Bruiser, but his biggest one was coming up next. Right now, they sat in second place overall. Boarlanders were in first and the Gray Backs were breathing down the Ashe Crew's neck for second.

"You should give him a lucky blow job," Drew suggested, waggling his eyebrows at Danielle.

She pegged him in the forehead with a grape, and Tagan snorted beside him.

Kellen frowned. "Is that a thing? Do blow jobs bring good luck?"

"Uh oh," Haydan said, rubbing his bald head, then leaning back on his locked elbows. "Skyler's got some work to do now."

"Shut up," Skyler said with a laugh. "No, babe. It doesn't bring good luck. It's just fun. You won't need my magic blow jobs to secure our spot in the relay."

"What's the relay?" Danielle asked.

Tagan draped his arm over Brooke's shoulders and answered. "The top two teams get to participate in the relay. The entire crew will each have a job, and the team who completes all the tasks first wins. If Kellen, Brighton, and Denison make good enough times on the Springboard Chop to qualify, we'll be able to compete against the other team in a relay of the events we've been doing all day. Winner takes home the trophy and a cash prize."

"And a pygmy goat!" Brooke squealed. She balled her fists and shook them in front of her like she couldn't contain her excitement.

Danielle's eyes went wide. "A goat? A real goat? Like a tiny, furry, cute, little goat?"

"Hey, good news for you, Denison," Bruiser said with a smirk. "Your mate loves animals."

"Shut up, man." Denison chucked a strawberry at his head, but he caught it in his mouth, the wanker.

"I'm your mate?" Danielle asked.

Aw, fuck it. "Yeah. That's what you are to me. I wanted to talk to you about it later, but these rats keep bringing it up, so yeah." His cheeks were burning like he was a schoolboy with a crush right

105

now.

Danielle leaned back, letting those chocolate-colored eyes go all hooded and sexy. "Are you calling me your girlfriend, Denny?"

"Denny!" the boys called out in feminine voices, among catcalls and whistles.

"Nah," he said, heat rushing into his cheeks. He was going to kill the guys for this. "You're more."

The smile fell from her face, and he looked away before he could see the rejection in her expression.

In a move that shocked him to his core, Danielle leaned against him and murmured, "Good." Then she pulled his knuckles to her lips and kissed them.

More shit from the guys rang out, but what did he care? His girl was grinning like he'd just made her day by locking down their relationship status.

An announcer on a bullhorn urged the Springboard Chop contestants to make their way to the logs set up in the middle of the grounds.

"You want that goat?" he asked against Danielle's ear, then nibbled it just for the excuse to feel that tender skin between his teeth.

Danielle nodded and blinked slowly, like his attention had made her drunk. God, he loved her sexy reactions to him.

"We're gonna get you girls that goat," he promised. "Kellen, Brighton, let's do this."

"Here we go," Tagan said, clapping.

Denison helped Danielle up, and she fed him her last grape, then dusted off the backside of her jeans. He gave that cute ass a squeeze and grazed his teeth against her neck. She shuddered, and he chuckled low. Oh, the ways he was going to make her say his name tonight. She'd been tormenting him all day in those tight jeans and being all cute as hell with her tiny kisses.

He slung his arms around Danielle and Brighton, caught between his two favorite people in the world as they made their way to the next event. Brighton was practically humming with pent up energy that would be expelled through the five pound ax they were about to batter the logs with. This event was the most physically grueling, and Kellen had already removed his shirt and handed it to Skyler. Brighton's team shirt went next, and Denison blew out his nerves in a puff of breath and reached over his head, then pulled the fabric away from his body.

Danielle's eyes went straight for the tribal tattoo

on his arm, and he grinned.

"Is that..." She looked up at him with such heartbreaking hope in her dark eyes. "Is that a badger?"

His grin stretched farther. He leaned down and kissed her lips. They tasted like sweet, ripe strawberries. "Maybe," he teased, then draped his shirt over her shoulder and jogged off without looking back.

EIGHT

That tattoo. Oh Mylanta, that tattoo!

Tribal symbols covered Denison's left pec and flowed into abstract shapes that formed what definitely looked like a fearsome badger on his shoulder.

Brighton stalled, smiling at her with his head cocked. He leaned forward, close to her ear. Close enough for her to hear his struggling whisper. "You've always been his."

Chills rippled up her forearms as he turned and walked away. Skyler and Brooke looked at her like she'd grown a floppy dong out of her forehead.

"Uuuh," Brooke said. "Did Brighton just talk to you?"

"Does he not talk to you?"

"Nope," Skyler said, shaking her head for emphasis. "That man hasn't talked to anyone since I moved to the trailer park."

"Oh." She watched Brighton's receding back. He was covered in curious scars, all perfectly straight from his spine to his side like tiger stripes, and aligned in rows like he'd been deliberately cut for decoration. "Maybe he talks to me because I'm Denison's girlfriend...er, mate."

"Maybe," Brooke said, following the others. Over her shoulder she said, "But I haven't seen him talk to Denison either."

Holy shit. Well, that was a revelation. Danielle suddenly felt honored that Brighton had chosen to share that whisper with her. He always swallowed hard after he said something, as if it hurt to make that much effort to push air particles past his vocal chords. But he'd still done it...for her.

The brothers climbed nimbly up onto springboards suspended halfway up the tall, vertical chopping logs, high up in the air. The boards bounced under them as they tested their balance. Kellen climbed up beside one of the Gray Back competitors and lifted his lip in a snarl.

Denison hadn't spared a glance at the Gray Back competitors until he was finished with each event. But right now, tension rolled off his shoulders when Matt took the log right next to him and stared at him with an obnoxious, empty smile on his lips.

"Come on, Denison," she said, clapping and hoping to hold his attention away from Matt's whispered taunts.

Brighton crouched down on his springboard, ax held out for balance like he was going to tackle Denison any second. It was the eyes. Denny was seething, the fury lightening his eyes to a snow white color.

Tagan was standing closer to his competitors and called out something sharp to Denison, but she couldn't understand what he said.

Denison's lips pulled away from his teeth as he pulled the ax out of his stump and turned his attention toward Matt.

Matt was already bending at the knees, like he was ready to brawl and get disqualified too, right here in front of everyone.

Aw, shit pills. "Denny!" she yelled.

He turned slowly as the announcer asked if the contestants were ready.

Danielle gave him a glare and angled her chin. "I want that goat, Denny."

He stared at her, and for a moment, she thought he couldn't understand the words she was saying anymore. Maybe he was too far gone. But when that whistle blew, Denny angled his body and sank the ax deep into the flesh of the log he was balanced on. Brighton spared one look of gratitude to her, then twisted his body with the blow of his ax. Rhythmic *chop, chop, chopping* filled the entire area, and the onlookers surged forward, crowding around this final event before the relay.

Boarlanders, Gray Backs, and Ashe Crew competitors were causing heavy damage to the logs, but Danielle found it hard to look away from Denny. His arms and torso flexed with each blow he sent shuddering through the log. His eight-pack rippled as he pulled the ax back out and swung in a graceful arch again. Full determination took his face as he set his stormy silver eyes on the task of demolishing the thick log with his ax blade.

The cheers from the crowd were deafening, drowning out the sound of the axes sinking into the splintering wood. Danielle was bumped and pushed forward, but she didn't care. Denison was beautiful, powerful...lethal. She'd never seen this side of him. It wasn't the sweet side or the protective side. This was fierce competitiveness and acute focus. The same hands that could pluck the most beautiful notes out of a guitar were gripping an ax and doing serious damage with each swing. His springboard bounced as he found his rhythm.

It was so close, she almost couldn't watch. She couldn't tell who was winning. Brighton, Denny, and Kellen looked to be neck and neck with the other crews. Onlookers were starting to chant the names of their favorite crews, and she joined in.

"Ashe Crew, Ashe Crew!"

Great goodness, she was proud of these boys. Skyler was jumping up and down beside her, chanting for Kellen, and Danielle couldn't stop the excitement that bubbled out of her throat as the boys got closer and closer to chopping through the wood. She chanted louder with the crowd and squeezed

Skyler's hand as they jumped together.

Denison gave one last powerful swing and his log buckled, then the top half caved. Kellen's went a split second later, followed by Matt's, then Brighton's. The onlookers were going wild around them, and she and Skyler faced each other and screamed elatedly.

They'd done it. They'd qualified for the relay.

The announcer called it, and Denison jumped from his springboard like he couldn't get away from Matt fast enough. As he weaved through the crowd, Danielle bolted for him. He crushed her to his chest as soon as he reached her and buried his face against her neck.

"I need a minute. I need a minute," he said low, over and over again.

Aw, crap. Danielle gave Skyler a helpless look and guided him through the crowd. Where were his sunglasses? She couldn't remember where he'd put them. Maybe they were still in the cup holder on top of the cooler near the lake.

The onlookers clapped Denison on the back as they passed, and his body vibrated with the reverberating congratulatory hits.

"It's okay, I'm here," she murmured.

As soon as they were free of the masses, she turned and pulled him toward the tents. An alleyway would be ideal, but just as she found one without anyone in it, she spied something even better. A dressing tent for the contestants had been erected. She dashed inside, but only one man remained in there, shirt off and texting on his phone from a bench against the white canvas wall.

"Out," she ordered.

The man looked up, then his eyes darted to Denison behind her, who was shifting his weight from side to side, looking down.

"Is he hurt?" Texty Fingers asked.

"He'll be fine." She jerked her chin toward the door. Hint, hint.

The man grabbed a gym bag and rushed out the opening. Danielle tied the three cords that sealed the tent flaps closed and turned just in time to catch Denison's hug. He lifted her off her feet and squeezed until she struggled to draw breath. She was finding it really hard to complain right now, though, because Denison was emitting a low rumble that lifted the hairs on the back of her neck.

"Shhh." Draping her arms around his neck, she

squeezed him and laid kisses across his forehead.

The scruff of his short beard brushed against her shirt, and her skin warmed as he exhaled a breath against the fabric.

"I can't stop...I can't," he murmured, not making any sense.

Whatever was happening was bad, and she didn't know what to do to help him.

Desperately, she lifted his chin to plead with him. His eyes were feral and reflected oddly in the dim light like an animal's. Unthinking, she lowered her mouth and brushed her tongue against his. He opened for her and cupped the back of her head. His kiss became urgent and needy, and suddenly, she was burning from the inside out. Whatever he was doing, whatever he was pulling from her, pooled instant wetness between her legs. It was instinctive, the need to be with him, something deep within her she was helpless to stop.

"Denny, please," she begged. Please what? She didn't know.

"Can you be quiet?" he asked. "I'll take care of you. Can you keep quiet if I touch you?"

"Yes," she lied.

He set her on her feet and yanked at the fly of her jeans, then shoved his hand into her panties and cupped her sex. She moaned as he slid his finger inside of her and pressed his palm against her clit. His kisses were hard, swallowing the sound.

His heartbeat raced under her hand as she rubbed the smooth skin there, and his nipple drew up into a tight bud under her touch. A delicious shiver began at the base of her tailbone and zinged up her spine until it landed in her shoulders. She loved Denny like this. Wild, barely in control, slits of snowy color every time he barely opened his eyes.

Encircling her waist with his arm, he pressed his finger into her harder and sped up the pace. She was already gone, floating to pieces, held together only by Denny's embrace. She didn't realize she was the one making the gasping sound until he shushed her softly and filled her mouth with his tongue, taking away her voice.

His bicep flexed with each stroke into her, and she tossed her head back as he drew an orgasm from her. Her body clenched around his finger over and over as waves of pleasure washed through her.

Denison let out a trembling sigh that sounded

nothing shy of relieved, and he relaxed his hold around her hips. He rested his forehead against hers and closed his eyes. When he opened them again, they were gray once more. Still too light to be completely human, but closer to his own color.

"I'm sorry," he said on a breath.

"Don't ever apologize for that. You just shared more of yourself with me than you ever have," she whispered, nuzzling her cheek against his.

He pulled his hand from between her legs and buttoned her carefully, then took his time making sure her shirt was straight and the hem perfect. He was stalling, and she smiled at how endearing it was.

"Are you ready to go back out there now?" she asked.

"Geez, Badger. You really want that goat, don't you?"

"I want the Ashe Crew to win this."

Amusement pooled in the soft color of his eyes as he searched her face. "That's my girl."

NINE

Danielle's head bobbed against the seat cushion with the uneven road. Her lips were parted slightly, her dark hair fanned across her cheek. Denison pulled his attention away from Kellen's taillights in front of his Bronco long enough to tuck her hair behind her ear so he could see her face better.

He'd been drinking her in since she fell asleep an hour ago. It was dark out, but the glow of the radio dials illuminated her face in soft blues.

The little gray goat lay in her lap, curled into a compact ball under her hands, staring back at him and apparently comfortable to just be still against

Danielle.

She'd always had a way with animals. She never met a dog on the street she didn't stop and pet, then rope the owners into a conversation about how cute their fur baby was. He'd taken her to a petting zoo when she'd been here before, just to watch her light up from the inside as she spent three hours petting every single animal. She'd named every last one of them and asked their keeper about their quality of life.

Denison sighed and narrowed his eyes at the sharp angle of a switch back he had to maneuver carefully to avoid going over a side rail and off a cliff.

Danielle liked animals, so maybe she could handle the snarling beast inside of him.

But what if she couldn't?

What if she ran?

It was too risky to share himself completely with her right now. He had to be patient. Had to wait until he was absolutely sure he wouldn't lose his mate again.

He'd watched Tagan after Brooke had left. His alpha had been forced to Turn the woman he loved, and she wasn't able to deal with it here surrounded by the Ashe Crew. She'd escaped to Boulder and spent months trying to control the grizzly inside of her. And Tagan had burned up, losing the connection with the enraged animal that sat just below the surface of his skin.

And Denison had burned with him.

He'd known that feeling—felt the ache of a mate loss. He hadn't been able to talk to Tagan or look at the heartbreak in his eyes without feeling sick to his stomach. Watching Tagan try to go on with life after losing Brooke had dredged up so many feelings about Danielle. Memories and a stark reminder of all he'd lost. He'd burned inside along with his alpha, but he'd hidden his sleepwalking and uncontrollable Changes. Nightmares of awful things happening to Danielle in some anonymous city where he couldn't get to her, couldn't save her.

When Brooke had returned, the relief Denison had felt was almost tangible. The nightmares had stopped, and the sleepwalking, too. He was able to put the pain away and lock it behind a set of iron doors in his mind. He could function again without being consumed with thoughts of his own lost mate.

Now Danielle was back, too. Denison had seen

the bond between Tagan and Brooke grow over the months, and he wanted that with Danielle so badly he was second guessing every decision he made with her.

He had to be careful about his timing, but he couldn't wait too long or she'd feel left out and leave like she did last time. Either way, he'd probably lose her.

Women didn't tend to stick around for this kind of life, and especially not human women. Choosing him back would mean painful decisions. It would mean deciding to become a bear shifter from his bite if she ever wanted to be truly claimed by him. It meant they would struggle to start a family, because history showed it was difficult for his kind to breed. She'd have to think long and hard about whether he was worth the pain and the constant care of the angry animal he would put inside of her, and then she'd have to decide if he was enough for her. If she could handle them being a family of two for the rest of their lives if he wasn't able to give her a cub.

Shit. He curved his spine over the pain in his stomach. Gripping the wheel until his hands hurt, he shook his head in the dark at the predicament he'd found himself in. He'd been a kid when he met Danielle, gangly and barely over twenty, and he'd allowed his bear to bond to her—to a human— without thinking of the consequences to her. He'd been so stupid, but love had ruled his life. His instincts had screamed she was his from the first time he'd met her, but he'd fought it. He'd tried to spare her at first. Spare her from his past and from the danger that lurked, snarling and waiting inside of him. But Danielle didn't get the name Badger for nothing. That woman had wanted him back and was determined to have him.

And he'd given in to her. How could he not? She was his mate, and he wanted to please her. Wanted to be with her and make her happy. Satisfying her had been the only thing that ever soothed the seething turmoil that constantly bubbled inside of him. It was bearable when she was near.

At twenty-one, he hadn't been strong enough to resist the idea that Danielle, the beautiful balm to his slashed-up soul, could be his for always.

He looked at her again and hated himself for what he would ask her to do. She looked so innocent and happy cuddled against the passenger's seat of his

Bronco, snuggling the baby goat.

It didn't matter that claiming her would be wrong, though, or that it would hurt her.

He already knew he would ask her because he was too weak to let her go again.

****

"I'm going to name him Bocephus. We can call him Bo for short," Danielle said sleepily as she handed the goat to Brooke.

The woman laughed and nodded. "That's a fine trailer park goat name. Tagan is setting up a pen for him behind our place for the night.

"Nighty night, wittle Bo," Danielle said in a silly voice as she scratched behind his oversize, drooping gray ears. "I'll give you a million snuggles tomorrow." She kissed a little white swirl of fur right between his eyes, then watched Brooke and Tagan leave with him.

Aw, she was going to miss Bo until tomorrow. She'd never had a goat before, though she knew a ridiculous amount of random facts about them thanks to her insatiable thirst for knowledge on anything furry, covered in tree bark, or plant matter.

When she turned around, Denison was looking at her with his lips pursed into a thin line. He almost looked…sad.

"I'm staying with you tonight," she announced, marching past him into his trailer. "The Airstream is too big and lonely."

His deep chuckle behind her sent chills of anticipation up the back of her neck.

"Badger, you're welcome to stay with me any time you want to."

He muttered something under his breath, and she turned. "What did you say?"

"I said you're welcome to stay with me—"

"No, after that. What did you mutter all quiet and sneaky-like?"

His nostrils flared as he inhaled deeply. "I said, forever if you like."

She moved to the couch in the center of the living room and leaned against the back to buy herself time to settle the flapping butterfly wings fluttering around her belly. "You'd let me stay here forever?"

Denison closed the door gently behind him, then leaned his back against it. "Of course I would."

She couldn't help the emotional smile that commandeered her face. "Today was the best day I can remember."

His gaze darkened and dipped to her tender lip. "Even though Matt hurt you?"

"Yes. He didn't ruin our day. Only a tiny part of it. You let me in a little today, and it was more than you gave me in the months that we were together last time. You've changed, Denison Donovan Beck. And for the better, if you ask me. I liked the boy you were. I love the man you've become."

He approached slow and slipped his hands around her waist, then bent down and rested his cheek against hers. As if he heard the cadence of music that wasn't there, he rocked them slowly back and forth in a dance that made her melt against him.

"Tell me more about what you like," he murmured in a soft stroke against her ear.

"I like that you are so devoted to your friends here. I like that you and Brighton are still close, and I like how you treat Skyler and Brooke. You boys revere them, always moving to take care of their needs before your own. You treated me like that today, and it made me feel adored and cared for. I like that you seem proud to have me beside you. That you don't mind that the boys give you a hard time over showing affection toward me. I like that you respect

Mother Nature. And Denny?"

"Yeah?" he asked, easing back to expose the deep happiness in his eyes.

"I like your tattoo."

"You think it's sexy, don't you, Badger?" he accused with a chuckle.

"Yes," she whispered, tracing his shirt where she knew the outline of it was. Running her fingertip along his defined pec, she smiled when he rolled his eyes closed and shivered under her touch. "But more than that, it's sweet that you did that for me, even after what I'd done to you. I hurt you. Hurt us both, and you still paid tribute to what we'd had. That says a lot about your loyalty."

He grabbed her hand without missing a step in their slow dance and kissed her knuckles. "You were always it for me, Danielle. It's the way it works with me. With everyone here. I could've never cheated on you like you thought. It isn't in my make-up. I only want you, for always."

She rested her forehead against his chest and tried to stifle the excited energy he caused when he admitted sentiments like this.

"I'm scared," he whispered.

Frowning, she looked up at him. "Of me? Why?"

"When this job ends for you, and you've done all you can do for research, I'm afraid you'll leave me again."

That didn't sound like what he'd meant to say. Denison was still holding back, but she understood. She'd burned him on the way out of town, and she would have to earn his trust back.

She stretched up on tiptoes and kissed him in a gentle promise that she was here to stay. Even when the job with Reynolds ended, she would find a way to work in these woods, near the man she loved. Near the man she'd always loved. She was going to put in the time and prove to him she wouldn't run when things got hard or confusing again.

She tugged at his shirt, scratching her nails gently against his skin as she lifted the hem, then tossed the fabric onto a heap on the floor. Still swaying her hips with his, she trailed little sucking kisses down his jaw and to his chest. She pressed her lips against the different shapes in his tattoo, then pulled his taut nipple between her teeth.

Denison muttered a curse as his hips bucked forward. Danielle brushed her fingers down his flexed mounds of abdominal muscles and pulled at the button of his jeans, then tugged the denim down his legs. His muscles twitched and jerked under her careful touch, and when she eased down the elastic band of his briefs, he inhaled in a gasp when her finger brushed the long length of his stone-hard erection.

He gripped the back of the couch until his knuckles turned white and his triceps bulged. His eyes were light gray now, not quite silver, but she would get him there. With a wicked grin, she knelt in front of him as he watched her with hooded eyes. The kitchen light was the only illumination, casting his flexing muscles into shadows and highlights. He was beautiful, bare in front of her, exposed, with that naughty smile that said he was utterly comfortable in his own skin.

Gripping the base of his cock, she teased his head with her tongue, tasting the drop of moisture that had beaded up on his tiny slit. Salt and Denison, and her stomach clenched with want.

He moaned and tensed his hips as she pulled him into her mouth, then eased back. In no hurry, she set a slow rhythm. She wanted to make him feel as good as he made her feel. She stroked him, careful with her teeth, lapping with her tongue until she could feel the veins go hard—until she could feel him swell in her mouth. Until he bucked against her and clenched her hair, guiding her. His stomach muscles strained, and he rocked into her mouth in shorter, faster bursts.

She touched herself outside of her jeans.

"Fffuck, Danielle, do that again." He leaned over and watched her cup her sex, then pulled his cock from her mouth. "Stop, stop, stop, I'm going to come," he rasped out, closing his eyes tightly.

"That was the point," she teased.

His lips were on her mouth before she'd even registered that he moved. He pulled her upward into his arms, hooked his hand behind her knees, and carried her to the bedroom as if she weighed nothing.

The room was bigger than she'd imagined, with quaint wainscoting along the walls, soft green paint, and old-fashioned sconces on either side of a plush looking queen-size bed, adorned with neutral brown tones and mannish sheets. Much nicer than she ever would've guessed for an old trailer in the middle of the wilderness.

Denison flipped on the switch near the door, and

a soft golden glow lit the room. Settling her onto the bed, he brushed soft, biting kisses down her neck before pulling her boots off and peeling her jeans from her thighs. Her shirt and bra joined the pile on the floor. The window unit air conditioner blew cold air across her skin, chilling her. With trembling fingers, she reached for Denison and smiled at the way he raked his silvery eyes from her lips to her breasts to her navel, then to the apex between her legs.

"You're beautiful," he murmured.

And right now, she felt beautiful. How could she not as he brushed his fingers down her ribcage and dragged his gaze along her collar bones, exploring her body. He wasn't rushing to satisfaction. He was adoring her.

Covering her body with his, he lifted up one of her legs and lowered his lips to hers. He canted his head and pushed his tongue past the closed seam of her mouth. Denny, her Denny, even tasted familiar from what she remembered. The head of his thick erection pressed against her wet slit, and she whimpered at the tease.

"You always were a noisy little thing," he

murmured against her lips. "I got off for years remembering how you used to say my name, all helpless, like you needed me inside of you."

He rolled his hips forward and his cock pressed into her deeper by an inch. Spreading her legs wider, she met his shallow thrust this time. He was propped on his elbows, trying to hold his weight from her, and his triceps flexed with every powerful stroke. Running her hands up the steely tautness of his muscles—the ones he'd earned doing hard, manual labor as a timberman, not a gym rat like she'd thought—she tilted her chin up and bit his lip hard to punish him for being too gentle with her.

He groaned as she moved for the tight cords of muscle in his throat and brushed her teeth against his skin. "Brooke checked my neck today to see if you'd bit me," she said. "I don't know what that means yet, but I think you wanted to earlier when we were together in your Bronco. You wanted to bite me then, didn't you, Denny?"

His breath came in short pants, and he thrust his full length into her until she was full of him, stretching around him.

"Didn't you?" she asked again.

"Yes," he gritted out. "I want to now, but I won't. Not until you understand what it means."

"Well, if you won't tell me, maybe I'll just bite you first. Where do you want it? Here?" She pressed her teeth over his collar bone.

Denison shuddered hard enough that his shoulders shook. He slammed into her, and she closed her eyes against the pleasure building inside.

"Or here?" she whispered, then bit harder onto the hard muscle near his tattoo.

His breath was nothing but desperate sounding gasps now as he bucked into her again and again. He closed his eyes, and teeth gritted, he let off a helpless sound.

She tested him, biting down hard enough that it should've been painful, but he pushed his chest toward her mouth, as if the burn brought him pleasure.

She bit down harder, close to piercing his skin, and he threw his head back as a snarl rumbled from deep within his throat. Over and over, he bucked into her until the pressure was too much. She released his skin and cried out his name as ecstasy pounded through her. Streams of warmth filled her as Denison froze and buried his face against her neck. He pressed into her twice more, then lay throbbing and spent across her body as she trailed her fingernails up and down his back.

And when his muscles relaxed completely and his eyes had darkened to a stormy gray again, he pulled the covers over them and cradled her in the crook of his arm. With one forearm under his head, he stared at the ceiling as she listened to his steady, drumming heartbeat that pounded a strong rhythm under her cheek.

His tattoo stood stark against the soft sconce lighting, a reminder that he'd loved her even after she'd gone from his life, and she traced the arcing abstract shapes there.

"Denny?" she murmured.

"Hmm?"

"Someday you'll let me in, won't you?"

He was quiet for so long she thought he wouldn't answer. His voice was deep and serious when he finally spoke again. "Someday I'll show you all of me. And then you'll run."

There was no use denying him when he sounded so sure of their fate. He was wrong, though. No matter what happened, and no matter what he was hiding, she wouldn't run again.

She hated herself for earning his distrust.

Around the emotional lump in her throat, she whispered, "I'm sorry for leaving."

His fingers combed through her hair, and he leaned down and brushed his lips against her temple. "I forgive you."

TEN

Denison rubbed the place on his chest Danielle had almost pierced with her teeth last night. Damn, he'd wanted her, too. Usually it was the male bear shifters who left a mark on their mates, but he and Danielle weren't like any of the pairs he'd ever met. He would've gladly bore her mark.

If she knew what it meant, that was.

Bo, the half-grown pygmy goat, followed Danielle around a giant pine tree like a puppy. They'd hiked for hours this morning as she collected bark samples from trees in various stages of beetle infestation. She'd taken water samples and packed vials from different ponds into a cooler she carried in a loaded backpack. He'd offered to carry the thing since it looked atrociously heavy for a smaller woman like her, but apparently she didn't need the help. She'd swatted his hand away and continued her mutterings about some kind of blue fungus.

The forest green backpack, he'd come to learn, was an entire portable library on animals and fauna native to this region.

Denison got why her boss wanted her to have a guide. She was plenty capable in the wilderness and was obviously a knowledgeable woodswoman, but she would've had to depend on topographical maps to find what she wanted. That and wandering around these woods on her own.

The realization of how close they were to the Gray Back Crew's current job site made him downright grateful to her boss for pushing the issue. He could hear their machinery from here, though Danielle with her dulled human senses likely wouldn't notice anything but the sounds of the woods. Sure, he missed the jobsite and working with his crew today, but at least Danielle was safe when he was with her.

He settled onto a fallen tree, nestled in patches of waving summer grasses, and watched Danielle take another measurement of the tree she was muttering to. It was cute that she talked to herself when she was working. Already, he'd learned more about the squishy green moss at the base of some of the trees than he had in his entire outdoor experience.

Pulling a long stem of grass, he gave a private grin as she bent down in one fluid motion and gave Bo a drink of canteen water from a tiny Dixie cup Kellen had given her this morning. Usually, he and the boys took shots out of those, but today, this one served as the goat cup.

"Can you help me cord this section off?" she called.

"Be happy to," he answered.

She'd been roping sections off all morning, then counting the affected trees versus the healthy ones for more accuracy. Then she would scribble the numbers in her notepad and likely use some formula later that would give her an accurate idea of just how devastated this forest was.

If he was honest, he was in awe of her knowledge of the area. He was an animal and learned by exploring and listening to instinct, but Danielle was smart. Book smart. She knew most of the plants and trees and knew scientific facts about each one. And if she didn't know something, she dropped down and flipped through her plant books, then repeated the name over and over until she committed it to memory.

Now, he wasn't a smart man, or an overly educated one, but he had other qualities about himself he liked just fine. He could play music and make people happy with his songs. He didn't have stage fright, and he was good with his hands. He had a strong back and could work big machinery on the job site. His alpha trusted him with just about everything up on the landing.

Danielle though—she had intelligence to go with her quick wit and happy demeanor. And he found that damned sexy.

He tried to focus on the task at hand as she tossed him the pre-measured loops of rope, but she looked good in her little forest ranger outfit. Khakis, thick-soled hiking boots, and a mud-colored tank top clung to her curves, and he couldn't for the life of him figure out if he liked her better in this getup or that sexy miniskirt she'd been wearing at Sammy's Bar.

His bear was practically humming under his surface with possessive happiness.

She was his.

Danielle just didn't know how thoroughly she'd been chosen yet.

ELEVEN

It had been six glorious days spent exploring the woods with Denison, and Danielle couldn't remember being any happier. She wished this job would never end. Perhaps if she did what Reynolds wanted her to well enough, he would extend her month-long contract.

She was going to ask him about it when she met up with him tomorrow.

Bo bleated from his oversize dog bed near the couch in the Airstream. The little hellion had gone to head-butting Denison whenever he got the chance, but he was sweet as pie to her. She loved him ridiculous amounts.

After tying the laces of her hiking boots, she grabbed her backpack and the stack of notebooks she'd filled with nature scribbles, drawings, and calculations, then opened the door and stepped out into the gray, early morning light. She waited for Bo to jump clumsily over the single stair after her before she closed the door.

The trailer park was immersed in chaos as the Ashe Crew readied to head up to the job site for the day. Denison had taken her up there yesterday and showed her around. She'd imagined all of the dangers of his job but hadn't really realized just how grueling the work was until she saw the crew working to drag logs up the mountain with that heavy machinery first-hand. She tried to keep her worrying to herself, though, because it was plain and obvious that Denison loved his job. They all did.

She waved to Tagan as he shoved a lunch pail into his truck. He smiled back, but it wasn't his usual greeting. Worry sat in his blue eyes. She only caught the glimpse of concern before he hopped into his big old black pickup truck with its heavily tinted windows.

That was weird.

"Hey, Danielle?" Brooke called from the door of the trailer she shared with Tagan. She was still in flannel pajama bottom pants and a red tank top she probably slept in. Her blond hair was mussed, and she looked pale, as if she wasn't feeling well again.

"Yeah?"

"Come see me after you go out with Denison today, okay? I want to show you something."

"Sure. I'll come straight over." Danielle frowned as Brooke closed the door behind her.

Something was up this morning. The usual rowdy greetings from the crew had been skipped, and everyone seemed on edge. Engines turned over and roared to life, and one by one, the trucks backed out of cracked pavement parking spaces and headed up the road that would lead them to the job site.

Denison stood bent at the waist as he rested his elbows on the railing of his porch. The megawatt smile he usually gave her first thing in the morning was missing. He didn't scoop her up and fondle her ass like he hadn't seen her for days either.

Warning bells clanged around her head, louder than the trucks that rumbled away and echoed off the mountainside.

"You need to leave Bo here today," Denison said as she approached.

"But...why?" She looked down at her little furry buddy, who was currently chewing on the cuff of her pants. She'd grown accustomed to having him and Denison around her while she worked. It would be strange collecting and pressing plants without the rascal trying to eat them.

Denison didn't answer, and a muscle twitched under his eye as he stared at her. He looked angry, and something more. Scared. What had she done wrong?

"Okay, I'll go put him in his pen."

After Bo was penned, fed, and his water dish changed for fresh, she closed the gate Tagan had constructed and shuffled toward Denison. She shouldered her backpack and hid her surprise when he crossed the street and headed to a small fence that surrounded the small trailer park. This wasn't the way they usually went to work, and she had a grid to follow.

Denison didn't say a word and didn't look back to see if she was following. And with every step she took on the thin trail that led up into the mountain that overlooked the trailer park, dread weighed heavier across her shoulders. Pressing against her more and more until it was hard to breathe.

The trail wound around ancient evergreens with trunks so large it would take two grown men to wrap their arms around them. The smell of sap and ozone filled the air, and above her, dark clouds churned and warned of an oncoming storm. The wind kicked up as she climbed over a boulder, whipping her hair this way and that until she gave up and pulled her dark tresses back in a high ponytail.

Denny didn't slow down, nor did he offer to help her up a steep embankment like he usually would. Perhaps he was still angry about her leaving and had decided she couldn't be trusted after all. She swallowed hard as tears stung her eyes from the thought of losing all she'd found over the last week. The endless days of joking with Denny and the nights in his arms. Feeling like she belonged somewhere for the first time. She thought of her friends and how badly it would hurt to leave them when Denny made her go. By the time she stepped into a clearing on the side of the mountain, she'd worked herself up quite capaciously.

Denny stepped from behind a tree and pulled his shirt off. His chest was heaving, as if emotion was choking him like it was her. He approached slowly, then hooked his finger under her chin and lifted her gaze to his. With a serious look that was completely at odds with the natural smile lines of his face, he murmured, "This is me, Danielle. Remember your promise."

Her eyes went wide, and she gasped as she absorbed what he was saying. Denison kicked out of his boots and jeans, then tossed them into a pile near the tree. Behind him was rolling mountains covered in pines and the gray morning sky. Above them, a giant bird screeched a call, and Denison stretched his neck up, watching it.

The first drops of rain spattered across his shoulders, and when he looked back at her, his eyes were the color of silver pond minnows. Flashing like the lightning in the distance.

She held her breath, afraid if she kept panting so hard, she'd pass out.

A smattering of pops echoed through the clearing, and his neck snapped backward. His form grew, and in a moment of disorienting confusion, a giant animal exploded from the man she loved.

Sand-colored fur covered every inch of him, and six-inch razor sharp claws the color of tar stretched from paws that were bigger than her face. His big block head shook back and forth as if he needed to rid himself of the last tingles of his transformation, and those silvery eyes she'd come to love watched her. His lips pulled back over impossibly long canines, weapons made for ripping and killing.

Her shoulders sagged, and she sank to the earth on her knees as he opened his mouth and let out a thunderous roar.

All this time, Denny, her Denny, had been harboring a grizzly bear inside of him.

****

Denison waited for the running.

He waited for the screaming.

Hell, he would've settled for a few curses tossed his way like Danielle usually flung into the universe when she was scared.

What he hadn't been prepared for was crying.

Shit.

He lowered his head and approached her slowly,

trying not to scare her any more than she probably already was.

Now she was sobbing, hiccups filling her throat as the rain came down harder on his mate. He didn't want that—hadn't meant to hurt her.

He was too riled up and scared to change back into his human skin, so he crept forward and emitted a low rattling noise, a worried question if she was a bear shifter and understood the language.

"I thought you were evil," she sobbed, throwing her arms around his neck.

Denison froze, utterly baffled as she clutched his fur in her clenched fists. If he wasn't mistaken, there were a few hysterical sounding laughs mixed in with her crying. Well, that couldn't be good. Right?

"Denny, you're not evil," she said, easing back and looking him right in his bear eyeballs. "You're a bear!"

Okay, Danielle was starting to sound excited.

Tagan had been preparing him for days for Danielle's reaction, but none of the scenarios included her hugging her boyfriend, the freaking grizzly, around his terrifying neck.

Clearly, Danielle had been grossly

underestimated.

He huffed a shocked-laugh sound and nuzzled her face until she giggled.

Relief flooded his veins, making him feel high as a kite. He'd smoked joints that didn't have this much kick. With a rocking motion, he scooped her up, careful of his claws near her fragile human skin, and pulled her against his chest.

She was hugging him tightly and laughing like a maniac, proving all his fears and nightmares over the past week null and void. He'd been wrong to be so scared of her reaction.

"Denny, Denny, Denny, my big silly bear. This is your secret?"

She clutched tighter to his fur, and he rubbed his face against her cheek, then moved to the other side, showing her just how much he appreciated her being such a brave mate.

"I thought you were a vampire! Or a zombie. But you're a werebear. How fucking awesome is that?"

Uh, not awesome at all until now. Mostly, being a werebear was a pain in the big furry ass.

She was sobbing again, shoulders shaking, and he hugged her tighter. And then she was...petting him. She ran her hands in long strokes down his shoulder blades as she cried against his fur. It wasn't the scared kind of weeping he would've understood. Her shoulders relaxed with every heave of raw emotion.

Danielle seemed relieved.

Closing his eyes, he tucked his animal back inside of him and slipped into his human skin again. She felt so good in his arms as she tucked her elbows in and snuggled against the now smooth skin of his chest. He kissed down her neck, tiny rewards for her being so understanding.

"You let me in," she said, pulling back and cupping his face. "You finally let me in on the big secret."

"I trust you." Denison's voice was raw, but that came from the pain of Changing back so quickly. "You didn't run."

"I told you I wouldn't. I don't care that you have a bear inside of you! I still love you, Denny. Maybe more now because you finally shared that part of yourself with me."

"Damn, Badger." He leaned his forehead against hers and closed his eyes, absorbing how good it felt to be with his mate and not hiding the biggest part of him anymore. She knew now, and she was still here. "I love you, too. More than anything. I was so scared I was going to lose you again."

"No, silly bear. You're stuck with me." She grinned. "Don't you know I love animals?"

He huffed a laugh and tucked a strand of damp hair behind her ear. "This isn't all of it, though."

"Tell me. Tell me everything and be done with it. No more hiding."

"This isn't a safe life." He gripped her waist to try to steady himself. Every time he thought about his past, his body wanted to seize and reject the memories. "If you choose to stay with me, you'll always be in danger. We don't live in a trailer park in the woods because it's our first choice, Danielle. It's safest for us here. We are freer to shift without being found out, but there are people who know about us. If you stay, you'll always have to be careful of everything you say to people outside of the crew. You'll always be looking over your shoulder."

Her dark eyebrows drew up with concern. "Who else knows?"

God, he wished he could swallow this down and

never talk about it. He'd never admitted this to anyone but Tagan. But he was dedicated to doing things right this time around with Danielle. He couldn't keep secrets and expect her to stick around for half-truths. He inhaled a deep, steadying breath. "When Brighton and I were sixteen, my parents left us alone for the first time to have a date night. I know that sounds extreme, but my family wasn't part of a crew. We were out there in the middle of the human population, trying our best to blend in, and my parents were protective. My sister had already moved out and joined up with a crew in Denver, but Brighton and I were still too young. We wanted Mom and Dad to trust us to be home alone again, so we weren't about to have a raging party or anything. Just some pizza for dinner, and we had a pool table, so I was planning on kicking his ass at that. But half an hour after Mom and Dad left, these men came for us. Black ops type, dressed in helmets and bullet proof vests... Shit." He scrubbed his hands over his face, not entirely sure he could do this without breaking down. Denison stood and kissed the top of her head, then moved toward the pile of clothes and began redressing to give him something to focus on other than telling this damned story.

"I don't remember much. Only flashes. White rooms. A man with black hair in a white lab coat and a surgical mask. A long hallway." He fastened the snap on his jeans and dragged his burning eyes to Danielle's. "Screaming. Mine and Brighton's."

"Oh, my gosh," Danielle murmured. She looked like she was going to be sick.

"I think we were sedated so we wouldn't Change, or maybe they did something to my head to erase what I'd seen, I don't know, but I have this nightmare. I get it over and over. I think maybe it's a memory. I'm walking down this hall, and I feel drunk, like my feet aren't really touching the floor. But I look in this window and Brighton is laid out on a table, strapped down while these two doctors are cutting into him. There was blood everywhere. Only, my brother isn't sedated. He's looking back at me, eyes wide like he can feel every cut they are making on him. And I'm burning, like I'm on fire, and my bear rips out of me. And I rip through these chains on my wrists and ankles and shred the two people who were walking me down the hall. And then I wake up. Every time."

"Is that what happened to Brighton's voice?"

Horror had transformed her face. Horror and devastation, and he could tell she was cut to her middle with his admission because she was wearing the same haunted look he'd seen in the mirror for the last nine years. He pulled his shirt on and avoided eye contact. Any emotional upheaval from her now, and he was done for. His throat would clog, his voice would shake, and his animal wouldn't allow such weak behavior. He'd Change again to avoid the pain.

Danielle approached and rubbed her hands up his back. He let her reassurance wash over him. When she wrapped her arms around his waist and rested her palms against his stomach from behind, he pressed his hand over hers to keep her there. Her cheek rested between his shoulder blades, and a warm, calming sensation spread from where she touched him, downward until his limbs tingled with the comfort.

"Brighton won't talk about what happened," he murmured. "He won't talk at all. They took his voice from him and scarred his body with their testing. He hasn't ever said it, but I think he remembers. It's an unspoken rule between us that we just don't ever bring it up. Brighton will disappear for days if I do."

Pain seared through Denison's middle as he remembered the awful years after they'd been taken. He'd been lucky enough to have been spared the memories, but Brighton had gone dim and became a ghost of his former self with whatever demons he was carrying. "When I came around, we were back home. Brighton had gotten me back somehow, but he was cut up real bad. We'd been missing for three days. Three days at the hands of people who knew exactly what we were. This would be your life, Danielle. You would be at risk if anyone ever found out."

"The others in the Ashe crew... are they like you, too?"

"All but Skyler. She's a falcon shifter, but she is one of us in all the ways that count."

"All the ways that count," Danielle repeated in a hushed voice.

Denison turned and rested his back against the giant evergreen, then pulled her closer, settling her between his splayed legs and against his chest. "I want to be with you. My animal chose you as my mate years ago when we were together. There was never going to be another for me because that's how it works. If a shifter like me is lucky enough to find a mate, it's a onetime bond. I have instincts, and they constantly urge me to claim you."

"Claim me? Is that the biting part Brooke talked about?"

"Yeah." He swallowed hard and hoped he had the right words to explain. "We can still be together if you're human. We don't have to do anything. We could stay just as we are. We could live the rest of our lives happy, just like this. There would be no bite, though. That would Turn you. I don't need that to be with you. It would hurt, and I don't want to hurt you. You should know how it is because the guys will bring it up."

"Are Brooke and Skyler claimed?"

Denison nodded slowly.

Her face fell, and she dropped her gaze to his tattoo. "I can't belong to the Ashe Crew if I'm not claimed by you, can I?"

His chest hurt as he watched the pain flash across her face. "Not as a human and not according to our traditions. But that doesn't mean you can't be with me and live with me. The Ashe Crew would still be your friends, even if you aren't a shifter."

"But I wouldn't be family. Not like you all are." Her soft brown eyes went round. "Brooke said it was hard to have babies. Would it be hard for us, too?"

He wished the answer was different. Wished he could put her mind at ease and tell her that someday he would be able to give her a cub. He wouldn't keep the truth from her anymore, though. From here on, she got nothing but honesty from him. She'd earned it. "It would be hard for us. Impossible maybe."

She dropped her chin to her chest. He'd dealt her a blow, and he rubbed her back in sympathy. He wanted to give her the world, not take things away from her. They'd never talked about having children, but she would make a wonderful mother. She was caring, sensitive, and had deep empathy, and the thought of never watching her swell with his child ripped his guts out.

"We don't have to decide anything right now," he murmured. "Even without the mark, you're mine, and I'm yours. I don't care if you stay human. You are my mate."

"Yeah?" She looked up, doe eyes brimming with moisture and full of hope.

If she only knew how deeply she'd burrowed

into his heart, she'd never be insecure about his devotion to her again. "Always."

TWELVE

How was Danielle supposed to settle down and have a professional business meeting with Reynolds and Darren after everything she'd found out over the past twenty-four hours?

Her mind was frazzled with the influx of information she'd absorbed. Vampires! Damn, had she been wrong. She'd made friends with a crew of badass, rip-roaring, protective-as-hell grizzly shifters.

She leaned over the steering wheel of her jeep and laughed out loud. Denison was a lumberjack werebear! Now *that* was sexy.

Sexy but dangerous.

He wasn't a danger to her, though. Every instinct she possessed screamed that he'd never hurt her. Even yesterday when he'd Turned in front of her, he was a gentle giant. He looked scary enough with his big barrel chest and powerful arms that shook the earth with each thundering step. But his eyes had been soft and sad when she'd been crying with the relief of finally understanding what he'd been hiding from her. No, he wouldn't hurt her, but rather he lived in constant danger.

She'd wondered why Denison hadn't gone big with his singing. Why he hadn't left this tiny town and made a name for himself. Anyone with ears could tell he was special with that clear baritone, natural affinity for musical instruments, and a memory for lyrics that stretched for miles. Now, she got it. Big dreams like that would be a risk for a man like Denison. It would expose him to more people and put his animal in situations he wouldn't be able to control. He wouldn't be able to hide his shifting eye-color or the snarl in his throat, and it would put all shifters at risk. So here he was, year after year, frozen in time as he played his weekly gig at Sammy's and plucked out tunes around the bonfire for his crew.

She was so proud of what he was, of the man and the bear he'd grown up to be while she'd been away, but that didn't mean he led an easy life.

What he and Brighton had gone through when they were teenagers was awful. Even if he didn't remember much of his time being tested on, she'd witnessed firsthand the devastation in his face as he told the story. No wonder Brighton didn't want to talk, not even at a whisper. His missing voice had to be a constant reminder of what had been done to him. If she chose to stay here with the Ashe Crew, she would have to learn to be overly careful to protect the people she loved.

She'd done as Brooke asked and knocked on her door after she and Denison had come down from the mountains. Brooke had showed her a beautiful painting she'd done of Danielle and a grizzly, Denison, sitting beside each other on the edge of the landing, looking out over the stars, sitting close to each other but not touching. Afterward, Brooke had sat her down and told her of how she had been Turned by Tagan at the cruel order of the last alpha. She had told Danielle about how he'd killed one of his own crew to save her and explained how hard it had been when she'd first been Turned. She had told her about how much it had changed her from the person she used to be. Danielle had already known what she would gain by joining the Ashe Crew—friends, family, and an unbreakable bond and sense of belonging—but Brooke had also let her know exactly what she would be giving up if she chose to allow Denison to claim her and put a bear inside of her.

She had a big decision to make, but she couldn't make it now. Not when her head was supposed to be wrapped up in this meeting.

There was an environmentalist outpost half an hour's drive from the Asheland Mobile Park. She hit the brakes and pulled to a stop in front of a dilapidated log cabin with overgrown landscaping. She tried to match it to her memories of the outpost from her internship here years ago, but couldn't. She frowned and checked the directions Reynolds had texted her again. *101 Pine Pass.* This was definitely the place.

A black SUV was parked alongside the house, and she stifled the nervous flutters in her stomach as she exited her jeep and gathered her notebooks. This would be her second meeting with Darren, but her first with Reynolds, and he was the one who held the power to extend her contract so she could stay here with Denison.

With a deep breath, she stepped around an empty, moss-colored birdbath and knocked on the front door.

"Come in," a man called from inside.

She opened the door and squinted into the dark room. The lights hadn't been turned on, and it took her eyes a couple of seconds to adjust after coming in from the sunny weather outside.

The cabin seemed to be one room and definitely not the outpost she remembered. In the middle of the floor was an old desk, polished to shining, and a high-backed office chair turned away from her.

When she closed the door behind her, the chair turned, and the man from the lumberjack competition, the one with the pitch black hair gone silver at the sides and cold hazel eyes, stared back at her with the empty smile he'd given her the first time they'd met.

"Mr. Reynolds?" Her voice trembled as frost blasted up the back of her neck.

"The one and only. Have a seat, Ms. Clayton. I do

believe you have some information I need."

"Right." The beetle infestation.

She folded herself carefully into the creaking leather chair in front of the desk and settled her stack of notebooks into her lap. Reynolds was wearing a black, three-piece suit, and more power to the man for dressing well, but this wasn't a corporate business meeting.

He gestured to her with an open palm. "Whenever you're ready."

"Aren't we waiting for Darren?"

He blinked slowly. "Darren isn't working for me anymore. He couldn't follow directions."

The way he talked down about Darren, as if he were a petulant child who couldn't mind rules, grated against Danielle's nerves. She hadn't liked the guy either, but when she'd initially met with him, he'd seemed professional enough and passionate about the environment here.

Reynolds lifted his eyebrows and clasped his hands on the desk between them, the picture of impatience.

Clearing her throat, she pulled a stack of printed notes from the front flap of her biggest journal. "I've printed off the most important findings for you as a quick reference for what I'll be talking about." She slid the paper-clipped papers across the desk.

Reynolds lifted his hands so she could push the papers under them, but he didn't look down at her notes. He only stared blankly ahead at her.

Uneasiness spread through her, making it hard to focus on the notebook she held clutched in her shaking hands.

"The infestation is much worse than previously thought," she began. "The beetles have demolished, or are in the process of demolishing, more than a quarter of the trees here already. Worse than the loss of the trees, though, is the loss of balance in the ecosystem. Native animals and insects that make their homes in and around these infected trees are already being affected. In small quantities, the pine beetles can be beneficial, serving to wipe out old and sick trees to allow for sunlight to reach the pinecones on the forest floor. But it has been so dry and hot in recent years and the forest is mostly made up of mature trees with fewer saplings that the beetle population has exploded. They use the bark to lay their eggs under, and they also introduce a blue fungus to the tree that slowly stops water and nutrient flow, eventually starving the tree. With the ongoing drought, the trees are already stressed and susceptible to the beetles. The land owner who hired crews to clear territory in sections is onto something. At this rate, the living ponderosa and lodgepole pines won't be salvageable and will sicken like the others at an alarming rate."

"Fascinating." The way Mr. Reynolds said it made it seem like he wasn't interested at all. "Now, share with me some information I could actually use. Tell me everything you know about Denison Beck and his brother, Brighton."

Shock slashed through her chest and sucked the air out of the room, congealing the oxygen in her lungs. "I was hired to study the beetle problem in this area. That is what I'm trained in, and that's the only reason I took this job. If you have questions about anything else, I can't help you."

Mr. Reynolds opened a drawer beside him and pulled out a stack of glossy eight by ten pictures, then slid them in front of her.

The horror and gore of the picture in front of her made her gasp and cover her mouth with her hands.

A woman in a lab coat lay on a sterile-looking tile floor, her stomach ripped to shreds and her throat torn out.

"You don't have to play coy with me, Ms. Clayton. I'm fully aware of what Denison is. I realize you likely feel an unnecessary loyalty to him, which is why I chose you to spy on the Ashe Crew."

She couldn't take her eyes away from the woman in the picture.

"You see, Denison is a murderer. So is Brighton." He brushed his palm across the stack, fanning out the gruesome images.

All featured a man or woman in a lab coat, their middles covered in crimson and unrecognizable as human anatomy.

"This victim of their savage rage," he whispered, pulling the last one from the stack, "was my wife."

The blond woman stared back at the camera with a blood-smattered face and glossy, vacant eyes. Even in death, she looked horrified.

But Danielle had heard the other side of this story, and a slow fury built in her veins. "Were you there?" she asked in a strangled voice.

"Yes. I witnessed their brutality firsthand."

"No, I mean," she gritted out, looking up, "were you cutting them and bleeding them and torturing them with these other *doctors*?" She spat out the last word like a curse.

A slow, cold smile drifted across his face. "I see you've grown sympathy for the plight of these animals, but I assure you, they are no more than servants to their instinct to kill. These doctors had families and homes. They had names and were real people."

"Denison and Brighton are real people, too. They have value, and you tortured them. Your team deserved what they got. They shouldn't have been experimenting on people. Blame yourself for what happened in that dungeon, you pompous prick. You kidnapped two innocent kids from their family. They were kids! And you cut them and bled them. You took strips of their flesh." A sob clogged her throat, and she gritted her teeth and swallowed it down. "You took Brighton's voice, and for what? What purpose did it serve to torture them?"

"We took Brighton's voice box to study how he was able to talk like a man and growl like an animal at the same time. It was a scientific enigma until we studied him. Our research has merit. We are able to study evolution as it's happening thanks to my research, you ungrateful cunt. You have no idea how valuable my work is."

"It's not evolution that is happening here! They aren't some super race. They aren't humans morphing into animals. Their genetic make-up hasn't changed since the dawn of man, so you're wrong. Your studies are worthless. They have nothing to do with you or me or where our species is headed. They are separate. Just a small group on the endangered list, trying to survive douche wagons like you who think you are superior enough to hurt people in the name of science. Fuck science, and fuck you."

She stood and spun for the door, determined to not say another word to this man. Denison and Brighton might have killed those people, but it was in self-defense after unspeakable things had been done to them. Whatever revenge Reynolds was seeking for his wife's death, Danielle wasn't going to be any part of it.

The crack of metal on metal sounded, and she froze, her hand on the doorknob.

"Turn around," Reynolds growled out.

She dropped the notebooks with a clatter on the wooden floorboards, then held up her hands in surrender as she turned and stared in horror down the short barrel of his handgun.

"Your little animal lover tirade doesn't matter in the grand scheme of things, Ms. Clayton. My team is already hunting your friends. I just needed you out of the way as my bargaining chip. Didn't want you getting caught in the firefight before I was able to use you."

"I won't help you hurt them," she whispered, tears of determination stinging her eyes.

"Then you'll die for them. For those animals."

"No," she said on a breath. "I'll die for the people I love. You're the animal."

Reynold's eyes went cold and vacant like the corpses in the pictures.

Then he pulled the trigger.

THIRTEEN

Son of a bacon sandwich, Danielle's arm felt like she'd shoved it in a bonfire. That dickhead shot her right square in the shoulder, and now she was bumping and bouncing around in the back of Mr. Reynold's SUV, pretending to be passed out.

Gritting her teeth, she wiped her bloody hand on her pants and pulled her cell phone from her pocket. *Dear goodness, let it be on silent.* She poked the home screen, and it switched over soundlessly. With a little huff of relief, she tried to call Denison. Three times it went straight to his voicemail without ringing, and she spouted off a string of expletives in her mind for the shitty cell phone reception at the trailer park and up on the job site.

Think, think, think. Reynolds said he had a team who were after the Ashe Crew, and she hadn't a guess if they were outnumbered or not. She did think they had guns, though, which would give them an advantage. Reynolds obviously knew what he was dealing with, and she doubted his team would show up unprepared with little puff pistols.

If anything happened to Denison...or Brighton or Brooke and her unborn baby. Or Tagan or Skyler or...

No, she couldn't think like that. She had to focus, ignore the pain fogging her mind and try to help them.

She didn't have anyone else's number in the Crew, not even Brooke's or Skyler's. She didn't have a single werebear number but Denison's.

And Matt's.

Grimacing at the pain in her shoulder, she searched for the number that buttface had plugged into her phone that first night at Sammy's Bar. The idiot had listed himself as Hot Matt.

Matt, she texted. *I need help.*

She held her breath, waiting. The cutoff for her

cell phone reception was coming any time now as Reynolds drove toward Asheland Mobile Park.

The cell phone vibrated in her clutched hand, and she closed her eyes in relief before reading the screen.

Who is this?

Danielle. Need your crew's help. Ashe Crew in trouble.

Are you fucking with me right now?

No! Researchers hunting us. Guns. Up on the job site. I've been shot. Please hurry!

If this is a joke, I'm going to kill you.

The bars on her cell phone dropped to zero, and the next text she tried to send came back failed.

The screen was covered in sticky red fingerprints, and she watched numbly as her now useless phone turned off. She'd done all she could do, and it hadn't been enough. Matt wasn't going to tell his alpha or show up to help. She'd watched the fierce competitiveness at the Lumberjack Wars. They were three separate crews, each watching out for their own.

She couldn't move her arm anymore. Couldn't feel anything below her elbow, really. The corners of her vision shattered inward, and she clung to the idea that she had to stay awake to help Denison. She had to do...something. Her vision blurred, then doubled, and she clutched her shoulder through the pain to try and staunch the bleeding. The carpeted floorboard was rough against her skin, and she tried to concentrate on the door handle on the back door—the one she'd tried to open four times now. Everything grew dimmer until she couldn't see anything at all.

Apparently, Reynolds was very good at trapping things.

****

"Rise and shine, Ms. Clayton. I have big plans for you."

Danielle cracked open her eyes as something stinging rang across her cheek, but everything in front of her was out of focus, as if she'd taken a shot the size of a fifth of whiskey. Pain burned down her arm and throbbed through her temple as she tried desperately to figure out where she was.

Reynolds was taking off his jacket in front of the opened back door of the SUV she was lying in. Her mouth dry as cotton, she struggled to prop herself up on her good arm.

"Faster, love. We don't have all day." Reynolds grabbed her shredded shoulder, blasting agony down her arm as he yanked her from the vehicle.

Her ears rang, and belatedly, she realized that awful screeching sound was her own screaming.

"Danielle!" Denison yelled, pulling her from the loop of confused anguish she'd been stuck in.

The scene before her would haunt her for the rest of her life, however short that might be. The machinery of the Ashe Crew's jobsite hadn't even been turned off, and it rumbled, drowning out any wood song from the forest beyond. A bear lay motionless except for the ragged rise and fall of his stomach in front of the processor. Denison and the others had been lined up along the edge of the landing with men dressed in black uniforms holding guns against the backs of their heads as they knelt in the dirt. Skyler was nowhere to be seen, but Brooke was crouched on her knees at the end with a bleeding gash across her temple. Tagan wouldn't look at Danielle, but something was wrong with his face. A constant stream of blood flowed from his chin. Kellen was beside him, eyes on his alpha as if awaiting an order Tagan didn't seem able to give.

And Denison... Half of his face was covered in red, and his jeans were stained dark on one leg. When he laid eyes on Reynolds, who was shoving Danielle toward them from behind, he went white as a sheet, and his pupils dilated to pinpoints. From here, his eyes looked completely silver. When he turned to Brighton, who was kneeling beside him, his brother wore a similar expression of horror and recognition.

Danielle wanted to kill Reynolds. She wanted him to pay for what he'd done to her bears. She burned to avenge them. Her anger mixed with the pain in her shoulder as he jerked her to a halt.

She struggled against him, yanking her ruined arm from his grasp, but cold metal pressed against her temple, and the crack of a gun cocking was deafening so close to her ear.

She bit her lip hard to stifle the oncoming tears and dragged her gaze to Denison's. He shook his head slightly in a silent order to stop fighting.

"So this is about revenge," Denison said, blinking slowly and bringing his hate-filled gaze to land over her shoulder on Reynolds.

"Oh, it's more than revenge. It's the end of a long,

satisfying hunt. I was happy to drag it on. To let you feel like you were safe up here in these mountains surrounded by people you thought could protect you from your fate, but I'm afraid my timetable has changed in recent months. I'm sick, you see. My disease is chronic and debilitating, and my doctor says I have only a few months to live. I need your bite, so killing you wouldn't reward me. It would doom me. And I'd like to think I'm a much savvier hunter than that. I studied the tissue samples we took from you and from Brighton. The regenerative properties were astounding. You baffled my team, and that's not an easy feat. We tried to sicken your tissue with every disease known to man, and nothing weakened it. So," Reynolds ground out, shoving the gun harder against Danielle's head as his fingers wrapped around her throat. "Who wants to do the honors?"

Danielle shook her head at Denison. "Don't. Don't give him a bear. He doesn't deserve one."

Reynold's grip tightened, cutting off her air completely, and she scrabbled against his hands with her fingertips.

"How about I count to three. I'd really like Denison or Brighton to do it, for old time's sake.

You'll all die for what Denison did to my wife, but if you are good little animals and give me what I want, I'll let this one go."

"He won't!" she gasped out. She was going to pass out again soon, but she'd be damned if the last thing Denison did was give this man what he wanted. Not for her. Reynolds had taken way too much from him already.

"One," Reynolds said.

Denison looked at his brother, and Brighton's shoulders sagged in defeat. His eyes had gone dead as he looked off into the woods behind them.

"Two."

Denison struggled to his feet, favoring his bloodied leg.

"Don't," she pleaded, struggling to drag air molecules to her suffocating lungs.

"Let her go first," Denison said in a tired tone that said he'd already made up his mind. "At least act like you won't chase her down the minute you kill us."

Reynolds chuckled, and she cringed away from the sound so close to her ear. He shoved her forward, releasing his strangle hold on her neck and said,

"Deal."

Denison caught her before she fell. "Run," he murmured against her ear as he settled her on her feet.

Her face crumpled as tears streamed down her cheeks. She knew what she could and couldn't do, and she couldn't walk away from her people. Not knowing what was about to happen to them. "I can't leave you like this."

"Badger," he gritted out. His voice dipped to a barely audible whisper. "I need you out of the way."

In the distance, an animal roared, and then another, the noise lifting the fine hairs on Danielle's arms. The woods filled with bellowing grizzly battle cries.

The corner of Denison's lip turned up. "You clever girl," he whispered.

"What the fuck was that?" Reynolds asked a pair of men with semi-automatic weapons trained on the forest behind them. "I told you to subdue all of them."

A giant falcon screeched from above them as she rode the air currents over the landing. Skyler.

Denison lunged at Reynolds as he brought the gun up toward the bird and wrenched his wrist until the clean *snap* of his bone could be heard.

"Now!" Tagan roared, his face morphing into something horrifying as the alpha spun and jerked the weapon out of his assailant's hands. Chaos and gunfire erupted. One by one, bears ripped out of her friends in blonds and browns, blacks and reds.

But not Denison and not Brighton. They fought human.

Denison hooked his fingers around Reynold's throat and slammed him down onto the ground with a sickening thud.

"Run!" he yelled, casting her a blazing look that dumped adrenaline into her system and got her legs moving.

Disoriented, she ran low, afraid of the zinging bullets as she made her escape. Ahead, a line of giant grizzlies was charging the clearing. A scream clogged her throat as they thundered past her without a single glance. Their gazes were murderous and intent as they joined the battle behind her.

"Oh my gosh, oh my gosh," she murmured, as she skidded to a halt near the Bronco and watched her friends fight for their lives.

The gunfire had ceased, and men's screaming

echoed down the mountainside. Fur and Teflon blurred until she couldn't make out anything in the pandemonium. She searched for Denny, and her heart faltered as she saw him dragging Reynolds out of the fray. Her mate was holding an ax and wore a deadly expression as he slammed the man who'd tortured him and his brother against a tree.

Brighton followed behind, and Denny didn't even look at him as he turned and tossed his twin the ax. Brighton caught it with one hand, and in a motion as smooth as river water, he pulled it back, rotated his hips, and slammed the blade toward Reynold's neck.

With a yelp, Danielle covered her ears and turned away before she could see the rest. That evil man had earned his death, but she didn't have to watch it.

When she dared to look back at the landing, it was all over. Bears were turning back to humans, and the team that had planned on annihilating the entire Ashe Crew lay scattered about the piles of logs and rumbling machinery.

Matt and his Gray Back Crew had come through, and when she counted heads, she realized the Boarlanders were here, too.

She sagged to her knees in disbelief that this had all happened. She'd been pulled from the SUV to find the Ashe Crew on their knees, but they hadn't been cowering to the men who had come for them. Their fearsome faces had said they were biding their time. They'd had a plan, she just hadn't known it. Pride surged through her that the crews had taken their territory back and fought together. They might've been competitors in the Lumberjack Wars, but when it came to real danger to others of their kind, they'd come running, no matter the physical danger to themselves.

Denison was crouched beside his brother near the tree line. Brighton was on his hands and knees. He had his fists clenched and was leaning hard on them, his teeth gritted as if he was in pain. Denison talked to him as he gripped his brother's shoulder, then rubbed his back, then gripped his shoulder again.

Brighton's pain gutted her. Twins had a special bond, and she'd seen the connection between them. That ability to say a hundred things without saying a word. They would share this pain together. Brighton rocked back on his heels and stood, embraced

Denison hard, and clapped him on the back. Then Brighton pushed away and stalked off into the woods.

Denny watched him go, hands on his hips and throat moving as he swallowed. He twitched his head, wiping his eyes on the sleeve of his shirt, then lifted his agonized gaze to her. He looked so vulnerable for just a second before he sighed and gave her a ghost of a smile.

A giant flapping of wings sounded, and a falcon bigger than any wild bird Danielle had ever seen stretched its curved talons out. As her feet hit the ground, her feathers disappeared and were replaced by human skin.

"No losses," Skyler said. "Drew took the worst of it before we were subdued, but he's already healing. We all are." She stretched her head to the side and flicked her dark locks out of the way to expose a long gash across her collar bone.

Good God, Danielle wished she could heal like that. If anything, her injury felt like it was getting worse.

Skyler knelt down in front of Danielle and ripped open the canvas hiking shirt she'd worn to the meeting with Reynolds. Danielle sucked air through her teeth and tried her best to ignore Skyler's stark nakedness. In fact, she was trying to avoid looking at the mass of naked, eight-pack wielding, big armed, tattoo-riddled men who were greeting each other and talking low in small groups on the landing. Only a few remained as bears, who meandered through the crowd.

Skyler made a clicking sound behind her teeth and turned Danielle's shoulder to look at the exit wound, which felt like hell.

"He got you good, didn't he?" Skyler lifted her bright green eyes to Danielle's and grinned. "Looks like you got marked after all."

"Yeah," Danielle murmured, confused, "but not by Denison. And it didn't Turn me. It doesn't count."

Denison was jogging toward them, limping less with each step.

Skyler lowered her voice and leveled her a look. "It does in my eyes. You took a bullet for us, and you called in reinforcements. The Boarlanders and Gray Backs were already on their way here before I even got to them to beg their help. That was you, wasn't it?"

Danielle nodded her head, too overcome with

emotion to find her voice.

Skyler lowered her eyes to Danielle's torn shoulder again. "You're Ashe Crew now."

Danielle's happiness at those words overpowered her insecurities. All those years feeling like she didn't belong anywhere dissolved away. The loneliness and fear of never finding her place in the world would be nothing but a dim memory now.

She'd found Denison, and she'd found her people.

Denison scooped her up in his arms and hugged her close. His whiskers scratched against her face, such a contrast to the soft fur he'd exposed to her yesterday. Man or bear, she didn't care at all, as long as he was alive and here with her.

Crying, she wrapped her good arm around his neck as he settled her into the passenger's seat of his Bronco. "Is it over?"

"It's all over. You're safe," he said.

The door shut so hard, it rocked the car, but he was rough because Denison was still riled up. She could tell because his eyes were too light.

"Is Brighton okay?" she asked as soon as he slid in behind the wheel.

"No. But he will be."

"He was the one who hired me, Denny. Reynolds planned to use me as his bargaining chip to be Turned this entire time. I think he's been watching you and Brighton all along. Watching me, too, even after I moved away. He followed my career and offered the perfect lure to get me back here." She explained everything that had happened on the way down to the trailer park, from the ad she'd found in the paper for the job, to the first phone call with Reynolds when he hired her, to the text messages she'd sent to Matt and her fear that he wouldn't respond to her plea for help.

And every time Denison took his eyes off the winding road to glance over at her, he looked so proud. It made her braver, made the pain in her shoulder easier to bear when he looked at her like that.

It was obvious seeing her hurt like this was hard on him. His eyes stayed fever bright the entire time it took him to draw a bath and gently scrub her clean. They remained silver as he cleaned the wound and stitched her up with a medical kit that made her wonder just how often bear shifters needed this kind of first aid. His eyes didn't darken to his normal stormy sky gray as he settled her onto his couch or busied himself with heating a gigantic pot of beef stew on the stove. It wasn't until the pain pills he'd given her kicked in and she leaned back and sighed in relief that he began to look like himself again.

The tension left his shoulders as he stretched out above her and pressed his lips against hers.

He eased away. "Are you going to leave?" Worry etched in a deep wrinkle across the bridge of his nose.

"Never. I'm not a runner anymore."

A soft knock sounded against the wooden frame of Denison's front door.

"Can we come in?" Tagan asked, though he was already halfway through.

"Come on," Denison said. "Dinner's ready."

So that was why he'd made that huge pot of food. He was feeding his people.

One by one, the Ashe Crew filed in. Brighton was missing, but she wasn't surprised. Denison had said he disappeared sometimes. He would come back, and she hoped that when he did, he could start to heal now that the man who'd hurt him was gone.

Haydan, Drew, Kellen, Skyler, Tagan, Brooke, and Bruiser all looked exhausted as they filed into the kitchen. Denison settled a steaming bowl in her lap, then leaned on the back of the couch above her, like her own personal sentry as he blew on a bowl of his own.

Danielle's arm was still throbbing with a dull ache, but as soon as Tagan touched the bandage with the brush of his fingertips, a strange warmth spread through her, numbing the stinging nerve endings. The alpha settled on the couch near her feet, and Bruiser touched her bandage next. Kellen followed, drawing a tremble of awe from her as the pain disappeared completely. Brooke watched with a curious smile on her face and a hand placed protectively over her stomach as Drew and Haydan touched her shoulder, then sat on the floor near their alpha.

This dinner was different from the boisterous bonfire meals she'd been sharing with them most nights. There were no jokes or laughter, no constant hum of easy conversation. There was only comfortable silence and a stark feeling of relief and gratitude. Today could've been disastrous, but they'd all survived it. Together.

For as long as Danielle lived, these bears would have her heart. And one in particular, the man who had waited for her to be ready for love, would have her soul. No matter what happened now, no matter what dangers lurked in this life she chose, she wouldn't go through it alone.

She had the adoration of the best man she'd ever known, friendship with people she respected deeply, and a sense of purpose here.

Denison looked at her like he couldn't believe she'd chosen him, but he had it wrong.

She was the lucky one.

EPILOGUE

Danielle sipped her drink as Denison pulled the microphone closer to his lips and dedicated his last song of the night to the "girl I love."

Pleasurable heat flooded her cheeks when he winked at her. She'd sat in the first row this time so he could see her under the spot lights. Also, so she could escape the swooning groupies near the bar in the back. It had been strange watching him perform without Brighton over the last few months, but hopefully his brother would come home soon.

Denison plucked clear notes from the strings of his guitar, and at last, he leaned toward the microphone and belted out the first lyric in his deep voice. This song made her emotional every time she heard it on the radio. It was about a man who loved a woman he deemed too good for him. Denison stirred feeling from her with just the first few lines, and she closed her eyes as his voice filled her.

Today had been perfect. He'd taken her into Saratoga on his day off and bought her lunch, then taken her to an action-adventure flick at the tiny cinema there. He even took her into a boutique and bought her a dress she liked. She'd worn it out of the store because he couldn't seem to take his eyes from the white, eyelet cotton material. She fingered the fabric that brushed her knees under the table and smiled to herself at how beautiful he made her feel.

Her life had undergone some major changes over the past few months. Damon Daye, the man who owned the Ashe Crew's land had hired her to keep him abreast on the thinly balanced ecosystem here. It had felt like a dream come true the day she'd signed a year-long contract with him. He was a good boss, and unlike Reynolds, was actually interested in their weekly meetings and her findings. He was a man who loved his land deeply. And while he was perfectly well-behaved with impeccable manners around her, she was also pretty sure he was a recluse and scary-as-hell shifter of some sort, but she hadn't figured out what yet. And every time she asked Tagan, he just smiled to himself like he enjoyed the secret too much to tell her. Once, she'd asked Tagan what had happened to all the bodies on the landing, and he'd told her Damon Daye had taken care of them, and that she didn't have to worry about it. She'd been too afraid of the answer to ask more about how Damon Daye knew so much about body stashing.

Beyond that, everything had fallen into place as she'd settled into the trailer 1010. She hadn't been able to stomach the Airstream after everything that had happened. She didn't want any reminders about Reynolds's violent mark near the trailer park. She even set up a pen off the back for Bo, who was now fifty pounds of gray furred, bouncing, climbing, gobbling naughtiness. He was also her companion when Denison was too busy with work up on the jobsite to go exploring the woods around her new home with her.

Every Friday night was her and Denison's time together, though. A day in town together, followed by his show at Sammy's Bar.

She felt someone watching her, so she turned and squinted at the bar. Matt sat there, nursing a beer. He lifted his drink in a silent toast, and she smiled, then raised her half empty cranberry vodka. He didn't bother her anymore. Not after the battle.

Denny sang out the last line of the song and thanked everyone for coming out. When the applause died down, he packed up his guitar into an old case and unplugged the amp. He grinned from ear to ear when she hugged him close and told him how much she loved the set he had picked tonight.

A few minutes talking to Ted at the bar and a wave for Matt, and they were loading up the Bronco and headed back into the mountains.

"I had fun today," Danielle said, rolling her head against the seat cushion to look at Denison.

He'd found his smile again after the battle at the landing. Especially today. Something was different about him, but she couldn't figure out what.

Like now, he was drumming on the steering wheel in a fast rhythm, as if he was playing a rock song in his head as he said, "Good. I had fun, too," in a distracted voice.

"You okay?"

More drumming. "Who me? Yeah, I'm okay. I'm great. More than great." His Adam's apple bobbed as he swallowed.

"Spill it."

"I don't think I should bite you."

Pain stabbed through her, and she shifted her shocked gaze to the road illuminated by the high beams in front of them. "You don't want me?"

"No, that's not what I'm saying. I mean..." He inhaled deeply and blew it out. "I like the way you are."

"Human?"

"Yeah." He slid his palm down her thigh and squeezed it reassuringly.

"But you said I couldn't be as close to the Ashe Crew if I wasn't a bear shifter." She wasn't trying to pout, but she liked the idea of being on the inside instead of the outside.

"What would you say if I asked you to marry me instead?"

Words failed her, and all that came out was a *wha* sound. Was he asking? This wasn't how she'd imagined this happening.

"Denny, claiming is a big deal for bear shifters. And I talked to Skyler. Exchanging tokens of affection is a big deal to falcon shifters. Proposals and weddings are special for humans."

A grin took his lips. "So you're saying if I ask, it needs to be somewhere more romantic than the front seat of my Bronco?"

She frowned and shook her head. "I can't tell if you're being serious right now or not. It's kind of a big thing to be joking about." And it was something she'd been secretly dreaming of over the past few months, so his teasing like this hurt.

She'd agonized over her decision to be claimed and Turned or not, but she was happy with the way they were, and the pain of the Change didn't feel necessary to prove her love. He had her—all of her—already. That didn't mean she didn't want something that bound them in tradition, though. And now he was teasing her.

Denison turned on the radio, and they drove in contented silence. She bit her thumbnail and stared out her window at the dark lodgepole pines they passed.

A strange glow flickered across the trees, and it

drew her attention to the front window. Straightening her spine, she leaned forward as her mouth fell open. Someone had doubled up on the strands of lights that served to brighten the trailer park at night. From here, she could see Asheford Drive as easily as if it were broad daylight, and everywhere, on porches and along cracked sidewalks, were glass jelly jars of flickering candles.

It was beautiful.

"What is this?" she asked on a breath as Denison put the car into park just under the Asheland Mobile Park sign.

He smiled and got out of the car, then jogged around front to open her door. He held out his hand, and when she slid her palm against his, he kissed her knuckles lightly.

The Ashe Crew waited at the other end of the park near the bonfire someone had built up.

"I've been talking to Tagan about this because I wasn't sure I wanted you to Turn for me. It doesn't matter either way, if you're human or bear." Denison pulled her hand into the crook of his arm and led her to the middle of the road. Slowly, he walked her down toward his people at the other end. "When we decided we were good the way we were, I still wanted more. I wanted a commitment that would tell everyone that you're mine, and I'm yours. So…" Denison turned and dropped down to one knee. He opened his palm, and on it sat a black velvet box that held a simple band of tiny, sparkling diamonds.

She laughed thickly as her vision blurred with tears.

"You're everything good about me," Denison said, searching her eyes. "Will you do me the honor of being my wife?"

Danielle drew her hands in front of her mouth to stifle her crying. This was way better than the front seat of the Bronco. Unable to talk, she nodded her head and caught his hug as he launched himself against her. Her shoulders were shaking, and she couldn't drag enough air into her lungs. She was crying all over his shirt as he lifted her up and spun her around, but she didn't care.

This was it. This was her mark. He was here, telling her he didn't need to bite her or change a single thing about her. He was here telling her she was enough, just the way she was, and she loved him deeply for it.

"She said yes!" Denison crowed as he slid the ring onto her finger.

She yelped as he lifted her over his shoulder like a sack of flour while the Ashe Crew cheered and whistled and catcalled.

"Denison Donovan Beck! I'm in a dress," she admonished, trying to keep her butt from hanging out for all to see.

He had his hand over the fabric, though, so she needn't have worried.

"That's right. A white dress. Your wedding dress."

"Wait, we're doing this now?"

"Hell yeah," he said, strutting like a proud rooster. "We've been planning this for weeks."

She twisted and looked at the smiling faces of her friends. "All of you were in on this?" she called out.

"Trust me," Brooke said. "You wanted us to be involved."

Danielle snorted and imagined what kind of good old country boy antics the crew had probably planned before Brooke and Skyler stepped in. No doubt this would be followed with copious amounts of boxed wine, slurred singing, skinny dipping and night muddin'. She loved it. She couldn't have planned a better wedding that suited her and the man she loved.

Denison smacked her soundly on the backside and settled her upright again. "We've just been waiting for Tagan to finish getting ordained."

She beamed up at the alpha and couldn't help the laugh that bubbled from her throat. "You're going to marry us?"

"We figured it would be fitting," he said, blue eyes dancing. "You'll be one of my crew now."

Her smile fell, and she stared at him as hope bloomed in her chest. "You mean it?"

The alpha tipped his chin up and smiled. "Skyler set the precedence for change by joining us as a falcon shifter. It wouldn't be fair to deny you because of what you are. Human, bear or pterodactyl, it doesn't matter what you are to us, only that from this day on, you'll be officially mated to Denison, which makes you one of my people."

She bit her lip hard against the onslaught of happy tears that fell from her eyes. Denison was claiming her tonight in a way they could both live with, and the Ashe Crew was initiating her as one of their own. The scar on her shoulder didn't matter. The years of insecurity and pain over the misunderstandings with Denison didn't matter. All that mattered was right here, standing in front of the people who meant the most, and reciting vows that would bind her to them for always.

And as Skyler and Brooke stood for her, holding bouquets of wild flowers and wiping damp lashes with tissues, she knew she'd stumbled upon a place as close to paradise as existed in this world. And her bliss was a rundown old trailer park in the valley of wild mountains with a timberman werebear who made her feel stronger than she ever imagined she could be.

Denison's nostrils flared, and he canted his head, ear to the woods. A slow smile crept across his face. Leaning forward, he whispered into her ear. "There's one last thing."

Danielle followed his gaze.

Brighton approached from the woods, back straight, chin up, eyes clear and looking much better than the last time she'd seen him at the battle on the landing. He made his way through the hugs and slaps on the back, then gripped the back of Danielle's neck and pressed his forehead against hers. He moved onto Denison and did the same thing to his brother. Then, he took his place beside her mate to stand in as his best man, and the Ashe Crew was finally whole.

Her heart was overflowing as Tagan began the ceremony.

Denison gripped her hands, steadying her, and mouthed, *I love you.*

His face was half in shadow as the glowing light from the bonfire illuminated the other side. His eyes were steady on her, full of adoration as he drank her in. Her strong, unwavering mate who'd waited years for her to come back to him.

Her heart was tethered to him so completely she would never feel like an outsider again.

She adored him, needed him. She breathed for his smile and lived for the sound of his laughter.

She beamed as her heart brimmed with happiness.

I love you back.

Want More of the Saw Bears?

The Complete Series is Available Now

Other books in this series:

Lumberjack Werebear
(Saw Bears, Book 1)

Woodcutter Werebear
(Saw Bears, Book 2)

Sawman Werebear
(Saw Bears, Book 4)

Axman Werebear
(Saw Bears, Book 5)

Woodsman Werebear
(Saw Bears, Book 6)

Lumberman Werebear
(Saw Bears, Book 7)

About the Author

T.S. Joyce is devoted to bringing hot shifter romances to readers. Hungry alpha males are her calling card, and the wilder the men, the more she'll make them pour their hearts out. She werebear swears there'll be no swooning heroines in her books. It takes tough-as-nails women to handle her shifters.

Experienced at handling an alpha male of her own, she lives in a tiny town, outside of a tiny city, and devotes her life to writing big stories. Foodie, wolf whisperer, ninja, thief of tiny bottles of awesome smelling hotel shampoo, nap connoisseur, movie fanatic, and zombie slayer, and most of this bio is true.

Bear Shifters? Check

Smoldering Alpha Hotness? Double Check

Sexy Scenes? Fasten up your girdles, ladies and gents, it's gonna to be a wild ride.

For more information on T. S. Joyce's work,
visit her website at
www.tsjoyce.com